PLAYING
the
FIELD

IVY BAILEY
PLAYING
the
FIELD

SIMON & SCHUSTER

First published in Great Britain in 2024 by Simon & Schuster UK Ltd

1 3 5 7 9 10 8 6 4 2

Simon & Schuster UK Ltd
1st Floor, 222 Gray's Inn Road
London
WC1X 8HB

Simon & Schuster: Celebrating 100 Years of Publishing in 2024

www.simonandschuster.co.uk
www.simonandschuster.com.au
www.simonandschuster.co.in

Simon & Schuster Australia, Sydney
Simon & Schuster India, New Delhi

A CIP catalogue record for this book
is available from the British Library.

PB ISBN 978-1-3985-3500-8
eBook ISBN 978-1-3985-3502-2
eAudio ISBN 978-1-3985-3501-5

Printed and bound by CPI Group (UK) Ltd, Croydon, CR0 4YY

MIX
Paper | Supporting
responsible forestry
FSC
www.fsc.org
FSC® C171272

For the Lionesses, who inspired the nation.
And for all the future Lionesses out there,
who refuse to give up.
You got this!

CHAPTER ONE

I'm packing up the last of my things when Mum knocks on the door.

'How's it all going?' she asks, strolling into my room and standing next to me to examine the neatly folded contents of my bag. 'Expertly packed, as usual.'

'I learnt from the best,' I say, putting my hands on my hips.

She reaches out to lift the football shirt at the top to check what's packed beneath. Finding more sports kit, she arches a brow.

'A long weekend at home and all you brought with you was football kit,' she remarks.

'What else would I need?' I tease.

She sighs. 'Sadie, I hope you're going to *enjoy* the rest of this term. It's important to have a bit of fun at university. You are in first year, after all.'

'What are you talking about? I've had a great time this term,' I say, puzzled.

'It sounds like all you've done these first few weeks is spend half your time at lectures and the other half training,' she says, before hesitating. 'Actually, let me correct that to one-third of your time studying and two-thirds training.'

'More like one-eighth studying,' I correct, grinning at her.

She gives me a look.

'I'm joking, Mum,' I insist, rolling my eyes. 'But, anyway, you're forgetting that football training isn't work to me. It's what I love. It's … everything.'

'That's what I'm afraid of,' she admits. 'I don't want you missing out on life because you're so busy kicking a ball around a field.'

I frown at her turn of phrase diminishing the sport.

'You know what I mean,' she says gently. 'I know how important it is to you – it is to me, too; it has been since I met your father – but university is about the experience and the people. You're allowed to have fun. Some of the best years of my life were when I was at uni in Manchester, and that's down to the friends I made there.'

'The team *are* my friends,' I point out defensively. 'I don't need anyone else.'

She gives me a wry smile. 'You sound just like your dad.'

My eyes flicker up to the framed newspaper cutting mounted on the wall above my desk. It's from 1989 and beneath the headline MCGRATH: THE TARTAN ARMY'S HERO is a picture of my dad on the football pitch with one arm punching the air, his head back and eyes closed in elation, as two of his teammates hug him round the waist, lifting him up off the ground. It captures the moment after he scored the last of his three goals for Scotland, winning the match and securing their place at the World Cup.

'I want to make him proud of me,' I admit quietly.

'He *is* proud of you – we both are!' Mum exclaims, her warm hazel eyes widening in horror that I might think otherwise. 'Sadie, you have been at Durham for just a few weeks and you've already made captain of the university women's team – the youngest in their history, thank you very much.' She prods my arm with her finger. 'What was it that your coach called you? Oh yes, their *star striker*. And to think you only started playing seriously two years ago!'

'Yeah, don't think I didn't hear you telling that to the guy who lives at number twenty-two when he passed you on the street the other day,' I remark, unable to stop a smile. 'I appreciate it, but I'm not sure our random neighbours care about stuff like that.'

'Excuse me, *everyone* should care about how talented my daughter is,' she insists, lifting her chin defiantly. 'And, if anything, that proves just how proud we are! But, Sadie, we're equally as proud of your achievements off the field as on it.'

'I know,' I murmur, nodding. 'But Durham has been champion of the National League twice in a row, and if we win for a record third time –' I take a deep breath in, irrationally worried that if I say this out loud, I might somehow jinx it – 'I might be scouted to play professionally. And for Dad to be there for that, for him to know that I can do it . . .' I swallow the lump in my throat, managing to add quietly, 'That's all I want.'

Her eyes glistening, Mum reaches out to gently push my hair behind my ear. For as long as I can remember, she's been encouraging me to stop hiding my face with my long auburn hair. I have the same colour hair as her, but while she has a shoulder-length glossy bob, I hate cutting mine, keeping it long and wavy. A shy, insecure child, I became adept at using it like a shield, keeping my head bowed and allowing my hair to fall forward over my face. The only time I ever have it tied back is when I'm out on the pitch.

That's the one place I'm not afraid.

'Dad knows you can do it,' Mum says, smiling warmly at me. 'Even if sometimes that slips his mind. In his heart, he knows.'

Feeling dangerously close to crying, I blink back the hot tears pricking at my eyes and step back from her. I clear my throat and turn my attention to my bag, zipping it closed.

'Right, I should get going, otherwise I'll miss the bus and then might miss my train,' I announce, lifting the bag off the bed and pulling its strap over my shoulder. I pause. 'Thanks, though, Mum. For the chat.'

She sighs. 'The house feels so empty when you're away. I have to keep the door to your bedroom firmly closed otherwise I find myself peering in, hoping you're secretly lurking in here somewhere.'

I chuckle, glancing round my box room, wondering where on earth I'd be able to hide in here. It may be small, but I love my room. It helps that I'm freakishly neat and tidy, and hate clutter, so it has a minimalist vibe to it and feels bigger than it is.

'You'll be home soon, though,' Mum adds, forcing a smile.

'Yeah, course. Just a couple of months until Christmas.'

'Maybe next time you might bring someone with you,' she says hopefully, leading the way out of my room onto the landing.

I groan. 'Oh god, Mum, don't start.'

'What?' she asks innocently, gliding down ahead of

me. 'Are you going to tell me that football and dating don't mix – is that it?'

'Something like that,' I mutter.

'Here she comes!' Dad announces cheerfully, appearing at the bottom of the stairs and beaming up at me. 'That bag looks heavy. What have you got in there, Sadie – the kitchen sink?'

'More like a hundred pairs of football boots,' Mum quips.

'Slight exaggeration,' I counter, setting my bag down in the hallway and finding my coat on one of the hooks by the door before pulling it on. 'Although I wouldn't say no to a hundred pairs.'

'Me neither,' Dad says, sharing a conspiratorial smile.

'I was only just telling Sadie that as wonderful as it is to be football obsessed – Lord knows, I married an obsessive – it's also important for her to *enjoy* herself,' Mum emphasises, giving me a stern look. 'She can't train with the team every night.'

'Ah, she's always been determined,' Dad says proudly. 'Once my Sadie puts her mind to something, that's it. No doubt about it. She was always a natural on the pitch.' He waggles his finger in my direction. 'I said you should have started sooner, but you were stubborn. I remember taking you for a kick-around when you were a wee lass and you wouldn't even try.'

'Because you took me for a kick-around with your *former professional* teammates,' I remind him. 'It was only slightly intimidating. I was scared of looking like an idiot in front of them! I knew all of them would expect me to be brilliant because I was your daughter. I didn't want to embarrass you.'

'Well, no matter, you got there in the end. I'm thrilled you're taking after your old man. Big shoes to fill, mind you,' he adds mischievously.

I smile at him. 'I'll do my best.'

'You need to go, Sadie,' Mum warns, checking the time. 'We'll say our goodbyes. We don't want you to be late.'

'Late?' Dad asks, his brow furrowed. 'She won't be late!'

'She will if we stand here huddled in the doorway chatting away for much longer. I want to make sure she gives herself plenty of time and, if she misses this bus, then waiting for the next one will give her very little time before her train.'

'She doesn't need to get the bus!' Dad declares stubbornly, turning to me. 'I'll drive you, Sadie. I appreciate you don't want to walk all that way with your heavy bag, so we can drive. It's no bother.'

Mum shoots me a concerned look.

'Harry—' she begins.

'The school is just round the corner,' he continues. 'It'll only take five minutes or so. Let me just find my keys.'

'Dad ...' I say, but he's not listening, busily patting the pockets of his trousers.

'Now, where did I leave them?' he mutters.

'Harry,' Mum says gently, reaching out to grasp his arm, 'Sadie isn't going to school. She's at university now. She's going back to Durham.'

He frowns, the creases on his forehead deepening.

'She left school in the summer, after her A-levels,' Mum continues. 'And now she's at Durham University, where she's captain of the women's football team. She's just come home to see us for the weekend, and now she's got to catch her train to go back.'

'Durham, yes, the football team,' he mumbles so quietly I can barely hear him. 'Of course. Of course.'

My stomach twists into a knot as I watch him struggle to find his bearings, his initial bewilderment replaced with frustration. After a while, he lifts his head to look at me, repeating the phrase, 'Of course,' through a weak smile, his brow still furrowed.

Mum rubs her hand on his shoulder and he reaches up to pat it gratefully with his.

One of the cruelties of dementia is how it comes in waves –one moment, everything is fine and your dad is teasing you affectionately like he always has, and the next moment, he's struggling to remember that you left for university a few weeks ago. It lulls you into a calm normality that it then shatters mercilessly.

Sometimes, when he's himself, I almost convince myself that it's not there; that the diagnosis was wrong and everything is okay. But then it comes back: the memory lapse, the disorientation, the panic and frustration.

As ever, Mum is the one to take charge of the situation while Dad collects himself, and I stand there numbly, plastering on a smile and feeling helpless. Reminding everyone that I'm on a tight schedule in her admirably chirpy tone, Mum encourages the goodbyes and, despite not saying anything out of the ordinary, I hug them a bit longer and a bit tighter than I normally would.

Mum understands.

'We'll be okay,' she whispers in my ear as I hold her.

After bustling me out, I hear her announce to Dad that it's time for a cup of tea as the door shuts, while I head over to the bus stop.

Marching down the road, I make a promise to myself to train harder than ever before, especially as our first fixtures of the season are looming. I am determined to make my dad proud of me on the football pitch before it's too late. Ever since he was diagnosed, it's been my dream to be scouted and signed for a career in pro football. I need him to see me achieve that, and nothing is going to distract me from that dream.

Sorry, Mum, but other life experiences will just have to wait.

CHAPTER TWO

Weaving my way through the crowd at Edinburgh Waverley Station, I feel my phone vibrate several times in my back pocket, but it's not until I've boarded my train and plonked myself down in my seat that I have the chance to check it.

DWFC ⚽🔥

Amy
Someone please kill me now
I've never been so hungover in my life
🏨😷☠️

Ella

I also feel like death

Who ordered those tequilas?

Alisha

Hayley

It was Hayley

I'm never drinking again

Maya

Hahahaha just remembered Amy dancing

on the stripper pole

Amy

OH MY GOD

I'd forgotten about that

I was wondering why my thighs had

carpet burn

Maya

Suffering for your art

Amy

They are red raw

Please tell me I at least looked good

up there

Maya

You looked GREAT

Amy

Are you lying to me?

Maya

No

Amy

I can tell you're lying

Alisha

I liked it when you hid your face behind

the pole and played peek-a-boo with the

people watching you from the dance floor

Amy

What.

What do you mean.

WHAT DO YOU MEAN I PLAYED

PEEK-A-BOO?????

Quinn

Morning, bitches

Wait

How is that the time?!

I'm meant to be meeting James for lunch!!

I'm SO LATE!!!

Maya

Quinn is late, everyone

Alisha

That is so new and surprising

Jade

Quinn

Fuck you all

Jade

Sounds like you had a good night! Sad to

have missed it

Will be out tonight tho if anyone's keen

Maya

Sounds good, hair of the dog 🍷

Amy

WHAT DO YOU MEAN, I PLAYED PEEK-A-BOO?!?!

Hayley

The tequila was a TERRIBLE IDEA

My bad

But if it makes you all feel any better, I

promise I'm paying for it now 💀 💀 💀 💀 💀

I'll be out tonight too ... 🍸😊🔥

Will try to meet up with you lot after 🍃xxx

I arrive at my dorms after a pretty smooth trip and go straight to my room to get myself sorted. I'm mid unpacking when suddenly the door to my halls bedroom swings open.

'Is she fucking kidding?!'

I look up from putting my clothes away in a drawer to see Jade standing in the doorway with a thunderous expression, holding her phone in her hand.

'Who?' I ask, sliding the drawer closed.

She strides across my room and slumps onto my bed.

'Oh please, Sadie,' she says in her clipped London tone. 'It's me you're talking to here. You don't need to act as though you're cool with it. I've been pissed off about this message for ages and desperate to talk to you, but I was at lunch with my parents and didn't have anyone to rant to about it. I'm glad you're back – I really missed you this weekend.'

'Same,' I say, smiling warmly at her. 'How was your parents' visit? Nice of them to come all this way.'

'Yeah, it was fine. They're big fans of the city. Dad kept lecturing me about the history of the place. You two would really get on, actually. He was disappointed that you weren't around to join us for lunch – he loves that I'm friends with a fellow history nerd.'

'I am not a history nerd. I'm just doing a history degree.' I laugh, shaking my head.

'And that's only because they don't offer a degree in football here,' Jade mutters, shooting me a knowing smile. 'Anyway, we had lunch at that tasting-menu restaurant and now they're on their way back to London.'

'The Michelin-star one?'

'Yeah. It was good,' she says, distracted by her phone.

I smile to myself. For someone like Jade, eating at a Michelin-star restaurant for lunch isn't that big a deal. An only child to hugely wealthy parents, she grew up in a beautiful townhouse in Knightsbridge, London, with holiday homes in Cornwall and France. With her glossy blonde hair, designer clothes, perfectly manicured nails and plummy accent, she is always impeccably turned out and genuinely intimidating on first impression.

She happened to be the first person I met when I arrived here at Collingwood College last term and I had a minor panic that I was stuck next door to a pompous, entitled posh girl, but I was wrong to judge her so quickly. By the end of our first night, I realised that she was so fun and warm and friendly that there was no way we weren't going to be best friends. The fact that she plays football too and qualified for the first team with me is an added bonus, and although personalities don't necessarily reflect position, it didn't come as a surprise to me that Jade is a talented defender. She's the most protective person I know.

'How was your weekend at home?' she asks. 'Did you have a wonderful time eating haggis and reciting Burns?'

I snort with laughter. Another reason I like Jade – she shows her affection by teasing. I've learnt that sharing emotion isn't exactly the done thing in her family, just as with mine. Taking the piss out of each other is how we work.

'Resorting to stereotypes is a very lazy form of humour,' I remind her.

'Whatever,' she sighs, before adding gently, 'Can we talk about Hayley now?'

Feeling a sharp pang in my chest at just the sound of her name, I lower myself into the chair at my desk.

'What about her?' I say glumly.

'Let's start with that fucking rogue comment on the WhatsApp group about tonight!' she exclaims, looking at me wide-eyed.

I shrug. 'She said she was going out tonight.'

'Yeah, with some very leading emojis that imply she's going on a date. Don't tell me you didn't think that, too.'

'Of course I did. I'm sure everyone understood that implication.'

'No one replied to her because they're all thinking the same thing: it's a dick move,' Jade seethes. 'She knows you're in this group. She knew it was going to hurt you. She did it anyway. Which brings me to my first question: *Is she fucking kidding?*'

Fiddling with the hem of my top, I look down at my hands.

It's my own fault. I shouldn't have got involved with someone else on the team. I was asking to get hurt. I noticed Hayley Ashton straight away. It would be impossible *not* to notice Hayley. She's tall and strikingly beautiful with her thick, dark curly hair, bright brown eyes and impossibly full lips. A second-year student who played on the team last year, she's confident and friendly, and she shot me a huge smile when the coach first introduced us. During that first training session, I scored a couple of goals and at the end she came running over to say to Coach, 'This girl is something special,' before winking at me. My heart somersaulted and my face flushed with heat. I couldn't think of anything clever to say.

When I made captain, I was nervous that some of the second-years might be pissed off that they'd been overlooked – there are no third-years in the team this year, so it's mostly made up of second-years and freshers – but Hayley made sure I was put right at ease, organising a surprise party for me in one of the local bars so that the whole team could celebrate my captaincy together.

'We all knew it had to be you,' she'd told me that night, leaning into me so she could be heard over the music, her soft, warm hand sliding down my arm.

'You're like no one else, Sadie. And we have every faith that you're going to lead us to another victory this year.'

She'd been so close, I could hardly breathe.

I knew that I had to shake off this crush. It was unprofessional and I couldn't be distracted on the field by one of my players. I was the *captain*. I had to be responsible. But I was too drawn to her, and when she made it known that she reciprocated my feelings, the temptation was impossible to resist. At first, we agreed to keep our fling a secret. While I'd made no secret of my bisexuality, she'd never even kissed a girl before and wanted time to process her feelings, and we both knew that it might not be good for team morale. Luckily for me, she didn't end up needing that much time to process it and the team turned out to be fully supportive – we spent so much time together on nights out, it wasn't exactly hard for them to work out what was going on.

It turned out to be too good to be true. After just three weeks, things started to cool off. She became distant and cold, and then when I called her out on it, she apologised and said she wanted to be friends. She justified it by saying that it had never been serious.

She was right. It had just been a few weeks and we'd never talked about being exclusive. We were having fun. I wasn't under any impression that it was anything more than what it was. But I had sometimes let myself believe that it *might* go somewhere. Dating someone like Hayley was exhilarating: she's smart and loud and fun – she turns heads wherever she goes. Being dumped by someone like Hayley is excruciating: she is the centre of attention, the life of the party, the glittering light that people are drawn to, while I have to lurk in the shadows, watching her like everyone else.

I know it was awkward for the team, but after our break-up I made sure my behaviour didn't change on the pitch and was sure to keep smiling and act completely normal around her when we were on nights out. When she flirted with guys in front of me, I laughed off the others' pitying looks and assured them that I didn't care. It had just been a fling!

I've been too convincing. Hayley happily flaunts her busy romantic life in front of me whenever she wants.

If anything, it gives me more motivation to focus on football only.

'Sadie,' Jade prompts now, her forehead creasing in concern, 'are you okay? Her sending that message is really unfair.'

'I've told you I'm fine,' I emphasise, attempting to sound casual. 'Me and Hayley are over. She has every right to date other people.'

'She doesn't need to put it in the group, though. That's ... *mean*.'

'It's only mean if she thinks it would hurt me, and I've told her that I'm over her. Just like she's over me.' I swallow the lump in my throat. 'Come on, Jade, we dated for three weeks. It's not like it was a big deal.'

'You were together every night for three weeks and at uni, that's like a three-year relationship,' Jade argues haughtily. 'Look, I get that you want to gloss over it and act all strong in front of the rest of the team, but I want you to know that if you want to talk about it, you can talk to me. Cry over her, rant about her, throw stuff at pictures of her – whatever makes you feel better, I'm here for you.'

'Thank you,' I say, smiling at her. 'But there's nothing to say. She's single. I'm single. We're friends and teammates. That's it.'

'I don't know why you liked her in the first place,' Jade says, wrinkling her nose. 'I get that she's pretty, but she's so self-obsessed it's jarring. She makes Narcissus look modest.'

I burst out laughing. '*What?* Jade! That's not true! You can't say that.'

'I can say whatever I like,' Jade counters, flicking her hair over her shoulder. 'She is not the big deal that she thinks she is, and you need to stop putting her on a pedestal. You can do so much better.'

'Sure,' I say sarcastically.

Jade arches her brow at me. 'Have you seen you? A flaming-haired Scottish beauty.'

I pick up a pen from my desk and throw it at her. 'Oh, shut up.'

'I'll prove it to you.' She laughs, dodging the pen and then throwing it back at me. I catch it in my left hand. 'Come out tonight and witness your fans drool. You can wear the dress I bought last week – it's a showstopper and will look incredible with your hair and that ridiculously toned body of yours.'

'I was thinking of doing some practice tonight,' I admit, glancing at the football in the corner of my room. 'There's a lot riding on our team this term. If we win the BUCS League, then we'll be—'

'Making history as the first team to top the Women's Premier North League three years in a row, blah blah blah,' she cuts in, rolling her eyes. 'Yes, thank you, Captain McGrath – I've been there for the ten million times Coach Hendricks has mentioned that. It's one night, Sadie. Come on, you've deserted me for an entire weekend. You owe me a night out.'

I sigh. 'Fine. Only for you.'

'Yay!' she cries, scrambling off my bed and coming over to throw her arms round me. 'Let's paint the town as red as your luscious locks! You won't regret it.'

CHAPTER THREE

The night starts out promising. Jade is on a mission – she poured the drinks freely as we got ready in her room with Beyoncé blaring, and the two of us set out tipsily for Osbournes bar in high spirits.

I'd felt apprehensive about wearing Jade's gorgeous but tiny low-cut black fitted dress, but the drinks had given me the nudge of confidence I needed to put it on and embrace the amount of skin on show, pairing it with my block-heeled black ankle boots and a leather jacket. A few of the football girls were at Osbournes already and, thanks to Jade announcing our plans on the WhatsApp group, they were waiting for us with a fancy bottle of Prosecco. Enjoying our drinks, we sit in our group, chatting and laughing until the music is too good to ignore and we have to dance.

I'm having such a good time that I forget Hayley is currently out on a date, until she shows up with him in tow.

'Oh my god –' Amy gasps in disbelief, staring at her as she weaves her way through the crowd in our direction – 'is that *Dylan*?'

Dylan Carson. The second-year goalkeeper and captain of the university men's team, and a renowned arrogant twat. His self-assurance isn't exactly misplaced – with his swept-back blond hair, piercing blue eyes and sharp cheekbones, he looks like he's stepped out from an Abercrombie and Fitch photoshoot – but his favourite topic of conversation is himself and he purposefully wears shirts a size too small to show off his muscles.

'I have to admit that I'd go there,' Jade once told me, eyeing him up during one of our joint training sessions as he celebrated a goal by whipping off his T-shirt and lassoing it round his head. 'But I'd hate myself afterwards.'

Their fingers intertwined, Hayley is leading Dylan towards us with a smug smile on her face, her eyelashes fluttering. They let each other go to greet their respective groups, Dylan darting over to a cluster of lads nearby while Hayley eagerly hugs some of the other girls. While she chats to Amy, she looks up and sees me, acknowledging me with a smile before her eyes flicker over to Dylan. He catches her eye and winks, a gesture that is noticed by his friends and prompts a round of merciless teasing.

'Dylan Carson,' Jade says in my ear, looking distinctly unimpressed. 'She's downgraded, I see.'

'He's hot,' I remark, before knocking back what was left in my glass.

'He's a classic rebound,' she says. 'She'll be bored with him by the end of the night.'

Hayley and Dylan don't seem bored at all; in fact they seem completely infatuated with each other. They spend the whole time whispering, giggling, kissing and dancing. I try to avoid looking at them altogether, but they don't make it easy, especially when they're locking lips so passionately that they stumble backwards into me, knocking me into Jade and causing her drink to spill.

'I'll get you another,' I offer quickly, noticing her thunderous expression as the two of them edge away from us, oblivious to the incident. I gesture to my own empty glass. 'I'm heading to the bar anyway.'

I join the back of the crowded bar, jostled by others trying to push their way to the front, and slowly shuffling forward as the poor bar staff rush around trying to keep up with the constant influx of orders. When I finally reach the front, I do my best to squeeze into a narrow gap and place my elbows firmly on the bar to cement my position, going up on my tip-toes, desperately trying to catch the eye of one of the staff.

After finishing an order, one of the girls behind the bar catches my eye and leans towards me. I've opened my mouth to tell her my order when a guy pushes his way into the tiny gap next to me, his elbow nudging mine over.

He shouts his order in an American accent. He winks at her. 'Thank you!'

I gasp in disbelief as the girl blushes under his gaze

and immediately gets to work on his order. I jab his shoulder with my finger.

'Um, *excuse me*,' I say loudly over the thumping bass. 'I was here first!'

'I'm sorry,' he says, looking me up and down and smiling. 'I have no idea how I didn't notice you there – a girl like you stands out.'

I narrow my eyes at him.

Okay, so I can see how that kind of unimaginative charm would work on most people. He's unbelievably hot – tall and muscular with a razor-sharp jaw and intense dark brown eyes. I'm actually going to forgive the bar girl for her miscalculation in serving him first. But I won't forgive him for cutting in, just because he's good-looking and knows it. Hayley and Dylan's PDA tonight, combined with how long I've spent queueing, has put me in a less than generous mood.

'*Please*,' I mutter, scowling at him. 'I was here first – you shouldn't have pushed in front. It's called common courtesy.'

'Whoa. Someone's having a bad night. We're out in a bar, having a good time! You should lighten up.'

You know when you're pissed off and the absolute WORST thing someone can do is tell you to *lighten up*?

'I was having a good time until you barged in!' I snap, knocking his elbow forcefully with mine to reclaim the bar space, causing his arm to slip.

'Jeez, here I was thinking the English were supposed to be charming,' he mutters.

I turn slowly to glare at him.

'*I'm not English*,' I say through gritted teeth.

He seems unfazed by my glowering expression and shrugs.

'Sorry. It's hard to hear you over the music,' he says, starting to nod his head to the beat. 'Don't you love this song? Ah, here she is.' He flashes a winning grin at the bar girl as she slides his vodkas over to him and then lines up the shot glasses, pouring the tequilas with flourish. 'Thanks, sweetheart.'

I grimace. 'Ugh. *Sweetheart*.'

He glances at me, raising his eyebrows. 'You're not a fan of "sweetheart".'

'No one is. It's condescending, overly familiar and

a classic use of linguistic power play to put women in their place.'

The corner of his mouth twitches with amusement.

'Is that right? Where I'm from, it's an affectionate term.'

'Sure, and you know this woman, do you?' I say, gesturing to the girl behind the bar. 'She's someone who you're affectionate with?'

He catches her eye and grins. 'Maybe we could be.'

Her cheeks glowing pink, she giggles.

'For fuck's sake,' I mutter under my breath, rolling my eyes.

'I'll tell you what, to apologise for my ignorant, sexist behaviour and for being better than you at getting to the front of the queue, let me buy you your round,' he offers. 'What would you like?'

'No, thanks,' I say, lifting my chin. 'I don't need your help getting served.'

'Come on, you don't need to be stubborn,' he says with a sigh, as the girl waits with the card machine, her eyes darting between us. 'What's your order?'

'I said, I *don't need your help*,' I repeat sternly.

'Fine.' He gets out his credit card. 'Have it your way. What's the damage?'

She passes him the card machine and he does a double-take at the amount.

'This can't be right,' he says, frowning. 'It's too little.'

'The shots are on the house,' she tells him, fluttering her eyelashes.

'Well, that is very kind of you,' he says, pressing his card against the machine and handing it back, before adding pointedly, 'Nice to know there are some charming people here in England.'

I press my lips together, ignoring him and keeping my eyes fixed on her.

'Hey, Dylan!' he calls out over his shoulder. 'Can you help me with these?'

Of *course* he's friends with Dylan Carson. It makes sense that dickheads would enjoy each other's company. As he passes the drinks back to his friend and then picks up the final few, he turns round and says, 'Good luck!' cheerily to me.

'I don't need luck,' I counter haughtily, but he doesn't hear me.

He's already weaved his way back through the crowd to the dance floor. The bar girl meanwhile has moved to the other end of the bar and is now busy serving someone else. Grinding my teeth in frustration, everything becomes a hundred times worse when, later on, I happen to catch the eye of The American as he makes his way to the loo. I'm still waiting to be served. He gives me a thumbs-up and then, cackling with laughter, disappears through the door.

I hate that guy.

'All right, gather round!' Coach Hendricks calls out, waving us over to the sideline of the football pitch. He's standing with Coach Nevile, who heads up the men's team.

It's the beginning of our first training session of the term and I've already been here practising penalties for forty minutes. Coach Hendricks got here just before everyone else and didn't say anything on arrival, simply standing at the sideline with his arms folded, watching me take the kicks and studying my form. He looked pleased, and as other members of the team began filtering onto the field, he sent them out to join me while we waited for everyone else, instructing our goalie, Maya, to take her position, and asking Amy, a fellow forward, to practise penalties with me. Maya saved two of Amy's and none of mine.

Giving Amy a high-five as I place the ball in the top right-hand corner of the net, we run over to Coach while Maya scoops up the ball in her hands and jogs up behind us.

'Bloody hell, Sadie, what happened over the weekend?' Maya chuckles, clapping me on the back as we reach the group. 'I've never seen anyone look so focused. The other Premier North teams don't stand a chance.'

My smile falters when I realise that Dylan and Hayley are standing in front of me and he's got his hand on her arse, pinching it. She giggles, slapping it away as she hisses, *'Dylan!'*

Although we mostly train in our separate teams, occasionally Coach Hendricks and Coach Nevile like the men's and women's first teams to practise together. Usually it's very satisfying, considering we beat them the majority of the time if we play a friendly match. While the university women's team is top of the league, our men's side is facing relegation.

'Right, almost everyone is here, so let's get started,' Coach Hendricks announces gruffly, running a hand over his buzz cut while Coach Nevile checks her iPad. 'Two laps of the field and then we'll set up for drills. Anyone caught slacking or gossiping will enjoy ten extra laps round at the end of the session.' He claps his hands, making us jump. 'Go on, then!'

You do not want to mess with Coach Hendricks. Broad-shouldered and muscular, he never cracks a smile and he speaks in a low-voiced growl that sends shivers down the spine. As everyone jolts into action, setting off on the first lap, he calls me over.

'Yes, Coach?' I ask, reaching him.

'We're depending on you to help us whip both teams into shape, Sadie,' he states, watching the group make their way along the side of the pitch. 'There's room for improvement in your team, and the men's team is in need of motivation. Their captain . . . well, let's just say he was the best of a bad bunch.'

Coach squints at Dylan, who slaps Hayley's bottom as he passes her. Telling him off, she launches into a sprint and overtakes him easily. We watch as he desperately tries and fails to catch her up again. I grimace.

'What do you need me to do?' I ask with a sigh.

'I'll let you know. I'm working on a plan,' he tells me. 'And the men's team may have had a stroke of luck. They've got a new player who seems promising.'

I frown in confusion. 'Someone has signed up this late?'

Coach Nevile nods, stepping closer to join our conversation. 'He came to speak to me a couple of days ago and I gave him a trial – he's good, lots of potential, so I thought there was no harm in giving him a shot. We'll see today if he can keep up.'

I scan the field. 'I can't see anyone new.'

'Here he comes now,' she says, glancing over her shoulder, back at the changing rooms. 'His name is Arlo Hudson. Moved here from over the pond.'

Turning to look, I recognise him instantly: the dickhead American from the bar the other night. As he jogs towards us, his eyes drift from the two coaches to land on me. I can tell he's trying to place me, and as he gets closer, suddenly it clicks. His face falls.

This should be interesting.

CHAPTER FOUR

'Glad you could join us, Arlo.' Coach Nevile checks her watch. 'Practice started five minutes ago. You're late. That's cost you five extra laps.'

'Are you serious? I got lost trying to find the sports centre. This campus is a maze,' Arlo justifies, putting his hands on his hips.

'Questioning your coach makes it six laps,' she says with a furrowed brow, while Coach Hendricks fixes him with an intimidating stare. 'Want to make it seven?'

Arlo shakes his head. 'No, ma'am.'

'Good.'

Coach Hendricks gestures to me. 'This is Sadie

McGrath, captain of the women's team. Any questions about the way things work here, go to her.'

'Wouldn't I ask the men's team captain, sir?'

Coach snorts. 'Sure, give that a try. Right, off you go, both of you. Two laps of the field and then we'll start on some warm-up drills.'

'We'll see what you're made of, Hudson,' Coach Nevile adds.

Leaving them to discuss strategies that Coach Nevile has up on her iPad, I start jogging and soon find Arlo coming up alongside me.

'We meet again,' he says, matching my pace.

'Lucky me.'

'Sadie. That's a beautiful name.'

'Thank you.'

I speed up a little, but don't succeed in shaking him off. To my irritation, he stays right at my side. I push myself to go faster.

'How was the rest of your night at Osbournes?' he asks, his breathing getting heavier.

'Great, thanks. How was yours?'

'I regretted those shots in the morning.'

'I bet you did.'

'You should have let me buy you a drink,' he insists. 'We could have got chatting and found out what we have in common.'

'What makes you think we have anything in common?' I breathe, speeding up.

He winces as he matches me and I can tell he's becoming uncomfortable now with this pace. Normally, I wouldn't push it this hard this soon, but my determination to beat him is fuelling my ability.

'We both like soccer, for a start,' he points out.

'Football,' I correct.

'Same difference,' he grumbles.

As we complete our first lap, he starts to edge behind me. Having finished their two laps, our teammates are sorting the cones and footballs for the drills. Dylan looks up as we pass him and yells out, 'Go on, Arlo! You've got this!'

It's not a race, it's a warm-up, but Dylan's idiotic cheer seems to ignite the inevitable competition between the two teams and shortly after his outburst, Jade shouts, 'Go, Sadie, go!' Soon enough, the two of us are sprinting round the pitch while everyone is yelling at the top of their lungs, the women's team supporting me; the men's team getting behind Arlo. Coach Hendricks watches on, bemused by the spontaneous race.

Arlo's support team gives him new life and he comes up alongside me once again, edging forward in a pitiful attempt to overtake. He's fast, but I'm faster. If anything, his challenge helps me find a fresh wave of energy. My legs work harder; my arms pump quicker. As we round the last corner into the final straight, I easily lengthen the gap between us, coming home to a winner's finish as my team jumps on me, clapping me on the back and cheering, while the boys are left groaning in disappointment, shaking their heads.

I turn round to see Arlo finish. As he comes to a stop and leans forward, bent double to catch his breath, I steady my own breathing, wearing a triumphant grin.

'Very entertaining,' Coach Hendricks remarks drily. 'I hope you two idiots have both reserved enough energy for the rest of the session. Hudson, we'll save those five extra laps you gained for your lack of

43

time-keeping for next practice. Why don't I see anyone lining up for drills?'

He waits for everyone to jump into action and Coach Nevile to move away before coming over to lean into my ear and add quietly, 'Good job, McGrath'.

'Thanks, Coach,' I say smugly.

Straightening and grimacing as he clutches at his side, Arlo glowers at me.

The coaches don't go easy on us today, the pressure of our first fixture looming. The training is gruelling and by the time we get to a friendly match to finish off the session, we're all knackered. Sometimes the coaches mix up the teams, but for today they keep it women's versus men's, and we win by a landslide. Arlo is a centre forward, but he finds himself with very little to do, thanks to the ball remaining largely in our team's possession.

At one point, one of his midfielders sends him the ball, but with growing pressure from Jade, he ignores his teammates' calls to pass to fellow forward Michael, and instead he takes a shot at the goal. Anyone can see it's a huge risk. No one is surprised when the ball goes at least a metre wide.

'Fuck's sake! What's he thinking?' Dylan cries from the goal our end, burying his head in his gloves.

It's hard to fight a smug smile.

Amy and I complement each other as forwards, and for the last few weeks we have worked relentlessly on practising our seamless co-ordination with the midfielders – Hayley, Alisha, Quinn and Ella – focusing on creating dangerous runs behind the defensive line. Just as we trained, Amy puts a perfect ball into the box for me to finish. As the ball soars over Dylan's head and hits the back of the net, Coach blows the whistle.

'Four–nil,' he concludes as we run in from the pitch to gather round him and Coach Nevile, who is standing next to him tight-lipped, scanning the glum faces of her team.

'Off you go, and next session don't waste our bloody time. Bring your A-game.'

As we all start to file off the field towards the changing room, he barks, 'McGrath! Hudson! Wait back a moment. We want to talk to you.'

I stop in my tracks, almost causing Hayley to walk right into me.

'Hey,' she says, glancing over to Arlo, 'what's going on with you and the new guy?'

'What do you mean?'

'Coach keeps bringing you two in for little chats,' she remarks.

'Not really. Just to introduce us, and I have no idea what he wants to say now.'

'But you already know each other. You were chatting at Osbournes,' she says, her forehead creasing. 'Arlo said he tried to buy you a drink.'

I hesitate, watching her curiously.

'You're right,' she says quickly, before I can respond. 'None of my business. Anyway, good game tonight. You . . . uh . . . you're playing better than ever.'

Dylan appears at her shoulder. 'Hey, babe,' he says, glancing at me and then nuzzling into her neck, which I can't imagine smells that good after an intense practice session, but whatever. 'Want to join me in the shower?'

She swats at him playfully, before offering me a small smile.

'I better go. See you later, Sadie,' she says, strolling towards the changing room while Dylan throws his arm round her waist and, judging from her giggles, obviously says something hilarious.

As I watch the pair of them walk away, Jade comes over, swigging from her water bottle.

'What was that about?' she asks.

'I'm not sure. She wanted to know what was going on with me and Arlo.'

'Ah.' Jade smirks, shaking her head. 'Jealousy rears its ugly head.'

'Her? Jealous of *me*?' I nod towards her and Dylan as they kiss before having to part ways to the different changing rooms. 'They're practically shagging on the pitch in front of everyone.'

'Yeah, I wonder why,' Jade says sarcastically, rolling her eyes. 'She's trying to get a reaction out of you.'

'She ended things with me, remember? Why would she bother?'

'Because she's confused. She doesn't want anyone else to have you, but she wants to make sure that you still want her. Her ego needs constant massaging. You moving on with someone else quickly isn't part of her plan.'

'Yeah, well it's not part of my plan either, so she can rest easy.'

'Maybe it should be,' Jade suggests, her lips curling into a mischievous smile. 'A couple of one-on-one chats with the hot new guy and you've sent Hayley into a spin. Think what you could do if you actually started seeing someone. You'd have her begging for you back like –' she clicks her fingers – 'that.'

'McGrath!' Coach bellows from where he's waiting with Arlo, startling both of us. 'You and Grosvenor better not be wasting my time by having a little personal chinwag.'

'We were talking tactics, Coach,' Jade claims.

'Good for you. Now bugger off, Grosvenor,' he says, before waving me over.

'I love your direct style, Coach,' Jade cries out, grinning widely at him. 'You be you.'

He narrows his eyes and Jade rushes off to the changing rooms, giggling. Not many people have the balls to tease Coach Hendricks, but Jade is one of them. She's not afraid of anyone and I love her for that.

Walking over to join them, I catch Arlo's eye.

Glowering at me, he looks away quickly. His face splattered with specks of mud from when he took an aggressive tackle from Jade and his shirt clinging to his skin with sweat, Arlo looks as though the last thing he needs right now is a pep talk. We wait silently as Coach Nevile discusses something with Coach, pointing out something on her iPad as he nods along in agreement. Finally he turns to address us.

'Thank you for hanging back,' he begins, rubbing his chin with his fingers thoughtfully. 'We wanted to run a proposition past you both.'

I glance at Arlo. He looks as puzzled as I feel.

'Hudson, it's clear you're a talented player,' Coach Nevile declares. 'You're fast, and what you lack in technical skill, you make up for in spirit. You don't have much discipline. And you take a *lot* of risks.'

'You got that right,' I mutter under my breath, kicking at the ground with the toe of my boot.

I think I'm talking to myself, but when I look up, I find all of three of them staring at me. I blush, pressing my lips together. Coach tilts his head, watching me curiously.

'You could learn something from that, McGrath,' he remarks.

I blink at him, stunned. Arlo suddenly doesn't look so miserable. In fact, his lips curl into a triumphant smile. Heat floods my face as I grapple with embarrassment and anger.

'Coach—' I begin, wondering if he's teasing me.

'We think it would be a good idea if you did some private training sessions,' he cuts in, getting straight to the point. 'McGrath, how would you feel about showing Hudson the ropes for a couple of hours a week?'

Arlo's jaw drops to the floor. I'm too gobsmacked to speak.

'You're not serious,' Arlo stammers, half-smiling as though he's missed the joke but knows it's there somewhere. He appeals to Coach Nevile. 'No way. You want her to *train me*?'

'Yes,' she says, dead-pan. 'With her help, you have a good chance at being a decent player and turning the luck of the men's team around. Wouldn't you say, McGrath?'

'I don't have the time to train other players,' I point

out, looking at them both in disbelief. 'I have to focus on my own game.'

'You're telling me that you don't think you improve your own skills and technique with a practice partner?' Coach muses, raising his eyebrows at me. 'You want my honest opinion, McGrath?' He waggles his finger at Arlo. 'This lad has the potential to be a brilliant player and I think that a bit of healthy competition might help in spurring you on to be even better. Not to mention, you might learn something along the way from him.'

I snort.

Arlo crosses his arms. 'Care to share the joke, McGrath?'

'Oh, just that it's hilarious to imagine I might learn anything from you,' I tell him, before turning back to Coach. 'You can't ask me to do this, Coach. I don't want to waste my time on someone who's not going to take this seriously.'

'Who said I wouldn't take this seriously?' Arlo says, glaring at me.

'I watched you out there today and you refused to listen to your teammates, you took risks that didn't pay off and, on the rare occasion you got it, you barely passed the ball. It's obvious you're not a team player,' I reel off.

'Oh yeah? I was watching you too, *McGrath*. You're boring,' he retorts.

I inhale sharply, taking a step towards him. 'Excuse me?'

'You heard me,' he retaliates, taking a step forward too, closing the gap between us. 'Everything is planned and executed with no personal style at all. Sure you can score, but can you score stylishly? No.'

'You know what? You have a lot of nerve to—'

'All right, cut it out,' Coach orders, waving his hands between us, forcing us to back up. Neither of us breaks eye contact, both too stubborn to be the first to look away. 'You can waste your own time with your petty back-and-forth, but some of us are grown-ups. Look, here's the proposition, plain and simple: McGrath gives you a couple of training sessions a week, Hudson, and you listen to everything she says and dedicate yourself to your improvement. You told Coach Nevile that football means a lot to you – now's your chance to prove it.' Arlo drops his eyes to his feet and Coach turns to me. 'McGrath, you would be out here training on your own anyway, so it's no skin off your back to have someone to train with. You can hone your own form, practise various formations, maybe come up with some new creative ideas. By helping him, you help yourself. Everyone is a winner.'

Concluding his monologue, he claps his hands.

'So, what do you say?'

It's a terrible idea. This cocky, aloof, infuriating person is one of the last people I would have picked to train with and the notion of him listening to a word I say seems laughable. He clearly thinks he knows better.

But against my own better judgement, I'm tempted.

Not just because Coach has a point – I would be spending my free time out on the pitch anyway, so a training partner would actually come in handy – but also because of what Jade said about Hayley being jealous. Whether I like it or not, Arlo has a lot going for him. Despite his obnoxious personality, sloppy form on the field and a complete lack of team-player mentality, I noticed several of the players checking him out earlier.

Just two chats with him in today's practice caused Hayley to ask questions. Imagine how she'd react to the news that I was giving the hot new American guy private training sessions twice a week.

Before I can get my thoughts in order, Arlo speaks first.

'Fine,' he says with a heavy sigh, fixing his dark eyes on mine. 'If you're happy to give the time, I'm in. It might be helpful to get some ... guidance.'

I find myself nodding. 'Okay. Let's do it.'

'Wonderful,' Coach says, lifting his eyes to the sky. 'Got there in the end. I'm proud of you both.'

Arlo brightens. 'Really?'

'No,' Coach claps back, scowling at him while Coach Nevile snickers. 'Witnessing you two bickering so pathetically made me question all my life choices that brought me to this moment. Now, go get changed before I change my mind about letting you off two more laps for boring me to death.'

We don't need to be told twice, the two of us racing away from the pitch and back towards the building.

'Sadie, wait,' Arlo says, stopping me as I reach the

door to the women's changing room. 'Are you sure about this? I think if this is going to work out, we have to be fully committed. Otherwise there's no point, right?'

'Right,' I agree. 'That won't be a problem.'

He nods. 'Okay, thanks. I appreciate you doing this for me.'

'You don't need to worry,' I assure him, before turning my back on him and pushing through the door. 'I'm not doing this for you.'

CHAPTER FIVE

He's late. I've been practising penalties for ten minutes when Arlo finally shows up at the pitch, strolling towards me without any urgency whatsoever. When I got back after our training session yesterday, I spent the rest of the evening coming up with a lesson plan.

And the dickhead can't even be bothered to arrive on time.

'Hey,' he says, coming over as I'm carefully setting the ball down a few centimetres left of the penalty spot.

'I thought you said you wanted to be fully committed,' I remark coldly, keeping my eye on the goal as I step back from the ball.

'I am,' he says indignantly.

'Arriving late doesn't give that impression.'

'Come on, Sadie.' He sighs. 'I'm a few minutes late.'

I carefully take my time to aim. 'If you were truly committed, you'd have been early.'

'I got held up on the phone to my mom,' he explains wearily. 'We don't always catch each other with the time difference, so it's hard to rush her off a call. It's not that big a deal, is it?'

'It shows a lack of respect,' I say, glancing at the ball and then back at the goal.

'Do you take everything this personally?' he asks drily.

'I take someone wasting my time personally when I'm trying to help them out.'

'It was *a few minutes*,' he's sounding irritated now. 'And can you *please* just take the kick before we die of old age? You're killing me here.'

Exhaling, I check my aim one last time before striding forward.

'Top right-hand corner,' Arlo mutters just as my foot makes contact with the ball.

It hits the net in the top right-hand corner. I turn to frown at him, hands on my hips.

A smile creeps across his lips.

'Told you,' he says with a shrug. 'I can read you like a book. As could the right kind of goalkeeper. You might want to try being a little less predictable.'

'I am not predictable!' I say defensively.

He snorts. 'You overthink everything and play it safe. I can see you analysing all the outcomes while you try to make a decision. All you have to do is kick the ball, McGrath.'

'I'm not here to take any advice from you, thank you very much,' I say curtly, seething that he guessed my play. He got lucky. 'You should warm up. I'd hate for you to hurt yourself when I put you through your paces.'

'Oof. I'm looking forward to it,' he says, winking at me before he sets off jogging around the pitch. I roll my eyes.

Ugh. He is SUCH an arsehole.

While he makes his way round his lap, I set out four cones into a square and pass the time waiting for him by doing some toe bounces. He eventually comes over and starts stretching. I accidentally glance at his toned, muscular arms as he does a shoulder stretch and my foot misses the ball, which dribbles across the grass away from me. He chuckles as I quickly go after it and scoop it up.

'Distracted by something you like the look of, McGrath?' he asks.

'In your dreams, Hudson,' I respond drily.

'Oh, you will be!' He grins.

I throw the football at him with some force and he lifts his hands just in time to catch it before it smacks him in the face.

'We're going to start with a basic dribbling square drill,' I inform him, gesturing to the cones I've laid out on the grass. 'It's a good warm-up and manoeuvring around these improves ball control and footwork skills.'

He looks unimpressed. 'Are you serious? I know how to dribble the ball, Sadie.'

'From what I witnessed, your dribbling was sloppy.'

'It was the first time I've played properly in a while.'

'Do you want to improve or not?' I ask impatiently.

'Coach Nevile told me to work on your focus and accuracy, so that's what we're going to do. If you have a problem with that, then you can tell her and I will *happily* give up on these extra practices.'

'Look, it's not that I don't appreciate what you're trying to do,' he says breezily, tossing the ball up in the air and catching it. 'I just thought we'd practise penalties, corners and free kicks and shit. Not do the boring drills they make pre-schoolers do. Coach wants me to be the team's lead striker, right? I think our time would be better spent if you get in goal and I practise striking.'

I sigh heavily. 'Arlo, how many times did you get a chance at goal the other day?'

He places the ball under his arm. 'I don't know. Once?'

'Yeah. Once.'

'Are you trying to rub it in that I messed it up?'

'I'm trying to highlight the fact that you can't wait around for your team to give you opportunities. You might need to create them for yourself. We need to get the ball to your end of the pitch before you have the chance to get it in the net.'

'And dribbling exercises are going to help that,' he says, unconvinced.

'Yes, Einstein. Keeping the ball close, being fully in control of it and changing direction with ease usually helps a player retain possession. You keep the ball; you get to shoot the ball. Got it?'

He tilts his head at me. 'You know what – you may be making sense.'

'Thanks for the compliment,' I mutter. 'So, as I said, we'll warm up with some dribbling and passing drills. See how you get on with those and then move on.'

'Passing drills,' he repeats, wrinkling his nose. 'Sounds boring.'

'You're in desperate need of them. Your teamwork and communication skills are seriously lacking.'

'I thought you said that you wanted to work on my dribbling so that I could keep possession of the ball before scoring,' he comments. 'The key word there being "I". What's the point in focusing on giving the ball away?'

'There's more than one player on a team, Arlo,' I remind him impatiently. 'You don't honestly think you don't need anyone else?'

'I think that if I have a chance at the goal, I'm going to take it.'

'What if someone else on your team has a better chance?'

He shrugs. 'I want to create opportunities for me.'

I stare at him, folding my arms across my chest. 'Wow. Maybe we should devote a large portion of our lessons to the importance of being a team player. It's the sort of lesson you offer young children at school, but, hey, guess you're a little behind on these things.'

'You're going to stand there and pretend that you don't think you're the most important player on your team?' He gives me a knowing smile before leaning forward and saying conspiratorially, 'Come on, you can admit it to me. I won't tell.'

'Oh my god, I can't believe I have to say this,' I mutter, throwing my head back in despair. 'Arlo, Lesson One: each player on a football team is as important as the other.'

'Say what you like,' he says, spinning the ball on the tip of his forefinger, breaking into a grin, 'but we both know that we are the ones who deserve all the glory.

That's why we're in this, right? That's why you devote all your free time to this game. So you can be the best. I know you, Sadie McGrath.'

I walk towards him and slap the ball away.

'You don't know anything about me,' I growl, looking up at him.

He fixes his eyes on mine. He doesn't say anything, his chest rising up and down with his heavy breathing. I swallow under his intense gaze. As his eyes flicker to my lips, I realise how close we're standing and I quickly stumble back, clearing my throat. I move to pick up the ball.

'We've wasted a lot of time talking,' I grumble, annoyed at myself. 'Do you want to do this exercise or not? I don't want to have to force you to be here.'

He holds out his hands for me to give him the ball.

'Let's give your way a go,' he decides.

I toss the ball at his feet. He drops his hands and stops the ball with his boot.

'Good,' I state, nodding to the cones. 'Get to work, Hudson.'

*

'You are *so* lucky.' Amy sighs dreamily, slumping back in the booth and taking a sip of her vodka cranberry. 'Why didn't Coach Hendricks ask me to give the new boy private sessions?'

'He is one of the sexiest guys I've ever seen,' Jade agrees, checking her cleavage in her low-cut pink top. 'And that American accent, too. *Gorgeous.* Where in the US is he from, Sadie? You must have talked a bit.'

'Not really,' I admit. 'I don't know anything about him except that he doesn't take instruction well.'

'He's from San Francisco,' Amy informs us eagerly. 'Hayley told me. I think him and Dylan are friends. His mum is Zimbabwean and his dad is American.'

'Did you get him to train topless?' Quinn asks, looking disappointed when I shake my head. 'Next time, get him to train topless and invite us to all come and judge his form.'

I roll my eyes.

We had our first league match yesterday against Stirling and celebrated our win with a fun night out that culminated in a terrible hangover this morning. When the girls wanted to continue the celebrations tonight, I was reluctant, but Jade managed to persuade me to join, especially as we've congregated in the Collingwood College bar. It's not like I've had to walk far. The girls have been pestering me for information on Arlo ever since Jade told them last night about our private training sessions, but I continue to disappoint them with my lack of enthusiasm.

Having started badly, our first session continued to go downhill.

Arlo is clearly still getting his head round the idea of being tutored by a fellow student because he hardly listened to a word I said, and when he did hear what I was telling him, he didn't take any of it seriously. It was as though the whole thing was a big joke to him.

It's incredibly frustrating because, if I'm honest with myself, there were moments when I could see what Coach Hendricks was talking about. Arlo can be ... well ... a little bit brilliant at football. When he wants to be, that is. He has a natural talent and there were times when he was dribbling the ball and running towards the goal that I could see a flash of something that I couldn't put my finger on – ambition, maybe. Dedication. A *passion* for it.

But then it would be as though something would shift in him. One moment I was watching a pro footballer, and the next, he'd lose the drive. He'd slow down, misstep, joke around with the ball, laugh it off. He would make it seem unimportant.

I can't work him out.

'Is he single, Sadie?' Amy asks eagerly.

'I don't know,' I reply, stirring my cocktail with its straw.

She blinks at me in surprise. 'You didn't ask him?'

'No,' I laugh, shaking my head. 'We were playing football, not chatting about our love lives. I think the less time chatting to Arlo, the better.'

'He can't be that bad,' Jade says, nudging me. 'He seemed perfectly nice when I spoke to him. Although, I couldn't actually tell you what he said. I got a bit lost in those sexy dark eyes.' She pauses. 'You know, I think Quinn might be on to something. Making him do a topless training session would really help boost team morale.'

'Our team morale is just *fine* without Arlo Hudson's help,' I insist.

'Is it?' Quinn shifts, sharing a look with Amy. 'How are things between you and Hayley?'

My face flushes with heat. 'Fine. Things are great. We're friends.'

'Yeah, but now she's hooking up with Dylan ...' Quinn hesitates, searching for the right words. 'I don't know – it can't be that fun for you to witness.'

'They're really flaunting their relationship, aren't they,' Jade remarks bitterly.

'It doesn't matter what they do,' I insist. 'They can do what they want! Like I say, Hayley and I are friends. The team doesn't need to worry. Look how well we worked together yesterday. We'd never let it affect our morale. I'm happy for her and Dylan.'

'And now, she can be happy for you and Arlo,' Jade says, smirking into her drink.

'We are *training* together,' I remind them all as the other girls giggle at her comment. 'That's it. Trust me, there is nothing but hostility between us.'

Jade shrugs. 'For now, maybe. But we'll see what

happens. I saw the way he was checking you out when you were running together.'

I turn to her in surprise. 'You're making that up.'

'I swear to god, he was checking you out,' she says with a mischievous smile, as she waggles her finger at me. 'I *knew* you had a thing for him. Look at the way your face just lit up at the idea of him being into you.'

'I did not light up!' I protest, downing the rest of my drink.

'She's blushing!' Quinn teases. 'You two would make a hot couple.'

'Agreed,' Amy says, before sighing wistfully. 'Although I would be a bit sad that such a hottie was off the market. I'm sure I'd get over it, though, and be happy for you.'

'Bloody hell, slow down!' I splutter, putting my empty glass on the table and jumping to my feet. 'Right, I'm going to get the next round of drinks before you lose your heads completely and start planning our wedding.'

Amy's eyes widen in excitement. 'Oooh, I wonder if you'd get married in America!'

'Amy!' I hiss as the others cackle with laughter.

'Who's getting married?' a familiar voice says over my shoulder.

I spin round to find Arlo Hudson standing behind me, wearing an intrigued expression.

'No one,' I stammer, my cheeks flushing as I ignore the sniggers coming from my friends. 'What are you doing here? You're not in this college.'

He nods his head towards Dylan and Hayley, who are at the bar with a group of the football lads. I hadn't seen them come in.

'Dylan messaged to ask if I'd want a drink – we're still drowning our sorrows after our loss yesterday,' he explains, craning his neck to see who I'm with. He smiles and waves at the girls. 'Hey, you're footballers too, right? I recognise you from practice.'

I step aside so they can introduce themselves properly, avoiding making eye contact with Jade and *praying* that he didn't overhear any of the conversation that he interrupted.

'Can I get you girls a drink?' he offers the group.

His adoring audience nod their heads gratefully and he takes their orders before turning to me last.

'And what can I get you, Sadie? Or is it bad form for an apprentice to buy their master a drink?' He turns to the other three. 'When I come back here with the drinks, you lot are going to fill me in on what she's said about me after our training, right?'

'Why would I have said anything at all about you?' I ask haughtily.

'Come on,' he says, bemused. 'You're going to stand there and pretend that you haven't been talking about me this whole time.'

The heat rises to my cheeks.

'I have better things to talk about than you, Arlo.'

'You break my heart, Sadie.' He grins, turning to look at Jade. 'She has said *something* about me, hasn't she?'

'Buy us those drinks and I'll tell you whatever you want to know,' Jade says flirtatiously.

'In that case, I'm buying you doubles,' Arlo says, much to her approval.

Flashing me a smile, he strolls off to join Hayley and Dylan at the bar.

I turn to glare at Jade to find her clinking her glass against Amy's and Quinn's.

'What are you *doing*?' I hiss at her. 'Now he's going to come back here and join us for the rest of the night!'

'You bet he is,' she says proudly. 'And when the time comes, McGrath, you better make me a bridesmaid.'

CHAPTER SIX

I'm so lost in my thoughts while tightening my bootlaces that I don't hear Hayley announce that Dylan has asked her if they can be exclusive. It's not until the rest of the team starts reacting to her statement that I tune in.

'Wow! When did he ask you that?' Amy says, her eyes flickering to me.

'The other night when we were all at the college bar,' Hayley says. 'That was the first time he asked, but since then he's been badgering me for an answer.'

'That's a bit soon, isn't it?' Quinn says in amazement. 'James and I were dating for a while before he asked if I was seeing anyone else.'

'Zara and I were exclusive after just a couple of weeks,' Maya points out with a shrug, before letting out a heavy sigh. 'Although, obviously, it turned out that she didn't really understand what exclusive meant . . .'

'It was a lucky escape, Maya,' Amy reminds her gently. 'You can do so much better.'

'Yeah,' Maya concedes, nodding. 'Lucky we weren't more serious, to be honest, before I found out that she was exclusive with another girl on her course.'

'She was awful, Maya,' Hayley agrees, tying her hair back. 'But I think Dylan is serious about us. Did I tell you guys that he showed up at the house yesterday with a bouquet of flowers? Completely unannounced. So sweet of him.'

'Yeah, you mentioned that,' Jade says, adding under her breath, 'a few hundred times.'

'So you are exclusive, then?' Quinn checks, pulling up her football shorts and grabbing her boots from her locker.

'I told him that I'd think about it and let him know,' Hayley informs us breezily, topping up her lip gloss in the mirror – something she's only started doing before practice now that she's dating Dylan. He seems to lick it all off for her before they start playing, so I'm not entirely sure what the point is, but each to their own.

'What do you girls think? Should I tell him yes?' Hayley asks, turning to address us.

I finish tying my boots and stand up. As I straighten, our eyes meet. I feel like I now need to answer her question, otherwise it seems as though I'm purposefully avoiding the conversation. I hate that she's talking about this in front of me, as though I was absolutely nothing at all to her and what we had didn't matter.

But I don't want her to know that.

'If you like him, then why not?' I say, plastering on a smile. 'I don't think it matters if it's fast. If you know, you know.'

Her eyes fixed on me, she nods.

'Yeah,' she says. 'That's what I think.'

Still smiling, I grab my water bottle, shut my locker door and head outside with Jade. Once we're out in the fresh air, I take a deep breath in.

'Are you okay?' she asks, her eyes full of concern. 'She's being such a bitch, Sadie. I don't know why she thinks it's appropriate to talk about shit like that in front of you.'

'It's fine,' I say with a wave of my hand, making my way towards the pitch. 'It's good that she feels she can. The more we act as though we're friends, the quicker we'll go back to being friends. The awkwardness will fade away.'

'I can tell that you're upset,' Jade says softly. 'You're allowed to be hurt, you know.'

I shake my head. 'It's not that. Well, I guess it is a bit hurtful. But that's not why I'm upset today. It's my dad.'

'Is he okay?' she asks, worried.

'Not really. I spoke to him on the phone earlier and ... he didn't know who I was,' I admit quietly, the words getting stuck in my throat.

'Oh, Sadie. I'm so sorry.'

'It's fine.' I take a swig from my water bottle, blinking back the hot tears pricking at my eyes. 'It hasn't happened before. That badly, I mean. His memory is getting worse and stuff, but I haven't ... He's always known me.'

Jade reaches out to grab my arm and slow me down to a stop.

'You want to talk about it? Or have some time to yourself?' she asks quietly, before nodding at Coach Hendricks a few metres away. 'I can tell him that you're not feeling well.'

'No, I want to play,' I say sternly.

'Okay, but if you want to talk—'

'I'm fine,' I say, cutting her off. 'But thanks.'

She nods in understanding and I race off into my first warm-up lap of the pitch.

I don't want to talk about it. I don't want to *think* about it. I've read a lot about this disease and I know that in a lot of cases it causes memory to deteriorate quickly. But I wasn't prepared for it to be this bad, this fast. This morning, I'd been on FaceTime with my parents, and Dad and I had been chatting about football – since I took it up seriously, it's been the best way for Dad and me to bond. He brightens at the topic and it's as though he's back to his normal self, enthusiastically talking about players and matches and tactics, remembering facts and scores from a long time ago that most people would have long forgotten. I'd been telling him about how Coach had asked me to train the newbie, and he'd been nodding along, intrigued by my lesson plans.

'Great – that all sounds great. You should talk to our Sadie. She's a keen footballer too,' he'd said, before turning to Mum. 'When is she back home? She might want picking up from the station.'

It was as though someone had punched me in the stomach and knocked all the breath out of me. My eyes filled with hot tears and my throat closed up. I'd smiled weakly as Mum had calmly explained that it was me, Sadie, that he was talking to now on the phone, and I watched the confusion etched into his expression as he peered at me on the screen again. It had been torture. I'd quickly made up an excuse to go. I couldn't bear to see him like that.

I just want to play football and drown out everything else.

'Hey, Sadie,' Arlo says, coming over when I'm stretching. 'Great night the other night. You have fun?'

'When?' I ask, watching Hayley greet Dylan with a

long, deep kiss, much to the disdain of both coaches hovering nearby.

'At the Collingwood bar,' Arlo says, frowning at me. 'You know, when we all hung out?'

'Oh, right. Yeah. It was fun.'

'Although anyone would have thought you were avoiding me,' he comments.

I turn to frown at him. 'What do you mean? I wasn't avoiding you.'

'Could have fooled me,' he says with a shrug. 'When I bought you those drinks, you sat on the opposite side of the table and barely spoke to me the rest of the night. I've been asking myself whether you purposefully avoided me because you don't like me or whether it's because you *do* like me. I'm thinking it could be the latter. Do I make you shy, Sadie?'

I roll my eyes. 'Don't flatter yourself. If we didn't speak all night, it was purely accidental. I didn't notice. I was having a fun night with my friends.'

We're interrupted by Hayley squealing with delight as Dylan lifts her into the air and spins her round, before kissing her again.

'Guess she agreed to make things exclusive,' Arlo remarks, chuckling.

'Guess so,' I mutter, before shouting over to Coach Hendricks, 'Can we play some football, please? What are we doing here?'

'Well said, McGrath.' Coach claps his hands. 'Today, we're going to play another friendly match: men's team versus women's. After your first round of league matches, it's clear that we need to— CARSON! ASHTON!' He shoots Dylan and Hayley a withering look as they remain entangled. They spring apart at his bark. 'You want to act like a pair of hormonal teenagers, do it elsewhere. This is a football pitch, not a school disco. Show some bloody respect.'

'Sorry, Coach,' Hayley says, biting her lip.

'Sorry,' Dylan echoes, waiting until he looks away to reach over and pinch her bum. She giggles and blows him a kiss.

The rage bubbles through me as their absurd PDA makes my bad day even more terrible. By the time we're instructed to get into position to play, I'm desperate to kick a ball as hard as possible.

'All right, Captains, in you come,' Coach Hendricks orders, waving me and Dylan over. He fumbles for a coin in his pocket while Coach Nevile places the football on the centre mark.

'You okay, Sadie?' Dylan asks, smirking at me as he pulls on his goalie gloves. 'You seem a little cross about something.'

He is the *worst*. What is Hayley doing with this guy?! Glowering at him, I can't wait to wipe that perfect smile off his perfect face when we beat them.

'It wouldn't be jealousy affecting your mood, would it?' he continues, relishing every word.

'Shut up, Carson,' Coach Hendricks barks, making Dylan jump.

Glaring at Dylan, Coach tosses the coin in the air.

'Heads!' Dylan yells.

Coach reveals the coin tails side up.

'Losers first, I guess,' Dylan remarks, shrugging it off.

'You really think *I'll* be the loser today?' I remark drily, stunned by his ignorance.

'Maybe not on the pitch, but I think it's safe to say

who's winning off it,' he says, before looking pointedly over at Hayley and waving at her.

She smiles back at him.

'*Fuck you, Dylan,*' I hiss, my self-control collapsing.

He grins triumphantly. Turning on my heel, I march over to the ball.

'You okay, Sadie?' Jade calls over.

'I said I was fine!' I snap.

I notice her share a look with Amy, but I ignore it. I don't care about anyone or anything right now except getting that ball in the back of the net. We are going to win this match no matter what. I refuse to lose again today.

Coach blows the whistle and the match begins – if you can call it that. Their team has no chance. We score in the first few minutes after Alisha sends the ball to Amy, who, seamlessly sidestepping her opponent, places it beautifully for me to break away from my defender. The ball soars over Dylan's outstretched hands and into the goal.

While Amy and I celebrate the goal, Dylan picks up the ball and chucks it furiously away, yelling at his team to 'do some fucking work'. Unfortunately, his inspiring words don't seem to have much effect – our defence line spends the entire first half bored out of their minds, gradually moving up the pitch just to get a touch of the ball. I notice Arlo getting more and more frustrated, working hard to support his defenders to no avail.

To give him some credit, he's by far the best player on their team, and at one point, when he finally secures the ball, he dribbles it confidently up the pitch only to lose it to Quinn, who puts pressure on him the whole time and eventually goes in for the tackle. He should have passed it sooner. If he'd done so, he might have had a shot at the goal.

When Coach blows the whistle for half-time, we're three–nil up. The boys are furious and we can hear Dylan telling them they're 'embarrassments' during their huddle. After glugging from my water bottle and tossing it aside, I'm making my way back onto the pitch when Dylan knocks into my shoulder as he goes to fetch his.

'What's wrong, Dylan?' I ask sweetly. 'I thought you

were prepared to be a loser on the pitch. Or can't you handle me beating you at anything?'

'The match isn't finished yet, Sadie,' Arlo reminds me, chirping in from where he's standing with the rest of his team.

'I think you'll find that it is finished,' I announce loud enough for everyone to hear, since we're all getting involved. 'You're hardly giving us a challenge. It will be miraculous for you to get close enough to even *score* next half, let alone win.'

Arlo gives me a strange look.

'Classy,' he mutters.

'What? You can dish it out, but you can't take it?' I ask haughtily.

'When did you hear me "dish it out"?' Arlo retorts. 'And it's never wise to start celebrating before the end of the game. We might be a bit rusty, but—'

'A *bit* rusty? HA!' I snort.

'Sadie,' Jade says in a warning tone.

'If we all played different positions, we could still beat you with our eyes closed,' I declare, spurred on by Dylan's thunderous expression.

Arlo folds his arms. 'Is that right?'

'In fact, why don't we?' I suggest, shrugging. 'Our forwards will switch with our defenders and we'll see what happens.'

'McGrath, let's not—' Coach begins, but Arlo cuts across him, stepping towards me.

'All right, fine,' he says, looking me up and down. 'If you're so desperate to prove your point, then why not? It will give me a chance to get a close-up look at your expression when I get the ball past you to score.'

'And it will give me a chance to see you face down in the mud when I take the ball out from under your feet,' I say, moving closer to him.

'Fine,' he growls, narrowing his eyes at me.

'*Fine*,' I say, refusing to back down.

After inhaling deeply through his nose, he finally breaks eye contact, turning to go and speak to his team. Glaring at his back, I do the same.

'I don't want to play in defence,' Amy groans. 'Sadie, do we really need to do this? We should be focusing on practising together for the next match, not proving that we're better than the boys. We already know that.

Leeds Beckett are a strong team and we can't go into that game feeling unprepared.'

'We're doing this,' I tell her firmly, before addressing the others, who are all watching me warily. 'See it as a good way of putting ourselves in our teammates' shoes. Sometimes it's good to get a fresh perspective on things. We might even get some new ideas for different, creative strategies.'

They look unconvinced, but I'm their captain, so they follow my lead. Coach Hendricks checks his watch and tells me I can do whatever I want, so long as I think it is genuinely helpful, which I assure him I do. Beating their team so easily and when we're not even playing in our positions is going to be a great confidence boost for us, I'm sure of it.

The second half gets off to a shaky start as we get used to our new areas of the pitch. Arlo even gets a good shot of the goal when, to my horror, Michael crosses it to him in the box and he heads it towards the top left-hand corner of the goal. It hits the crossbar and bounces over the top of the net out of play, leaving him burying his head in his hands and me breathing a sigh of relief.

After that shock, I stop acting quite so complacent and yell at my team to remain focused. We win back possession and, a few minutes later, Quinn sends it to Alisha, who puts the ball in the back of the net, causing Dylan to shout a list of expletives. I continue to stay on Arlo, applying as much pressure as possible when he's passed the ball again, and this time I'm not going to let him have another chance. As he tries to speed away from me, I ruthlessly tackle him with a lot more effort than is necessary, causing his legs to go out from under him. He slams onto the ground and I pass the ball away, cackling with laughter. Pushing himself up onto his elbows, he shoots me a look – it's pure loathing.

Coach blows the whistle to signal the end of the session and I reach out to help Arlo up, but he refuses my offer, swatting my hand away and getting to his feet as one of his teammates comes over to give him a comforting pat on the back. He storms off the pitch towards the changing rooms, followed by the rest of his team. I'm surprised to find none of my team celebrating. Even Jade looks uncomfortable.

'Interesting play there, McGrath,' Coach Hendricks comments, frowning at me.

'I didn't foul him,' I say defensively, throwing up my hands in exasperation. 'It's not my fault he couldn't take the pressure.'

'I asked you to train him so that you could give his team a newfound confidence and make them believe they can win,' Coach Hendricks reminds me gruffly. 'Not go out of your way to humiliate him and tear the rest of them down.'

With that, he turns his back on me and I stand on the pitch alone, watching him and the rest of my team walk away.

CHAPTER SEVEN

When Arlo doesn't show up to our private training session the next day, I decide to seek him out. At first I felt that Coach had been unfair – we won that match fair and square, and Arlo agreed to let us switch positions, so I didn't feel entirely to blame for his embarrassment. But there was no gloating in our changing room after the session and I couldn't miss the dirty looks Hayley shot me when she went to comfort Dylan after. Even Jade commented that, though she was on my side and she loved Dylan being knocked down a few pegs, she felt that I'd been a little too brutal.

'You'd had a tough day,' she'd justified, smiling at me. 'Come on, let's go get a drink.'

I'd refused the drink and gone back to my room to study some football formations on YouTube, but the guilt had started to seep in and I'd decided to apologise to Arlo today when I got him on his own.

I suppose I shouldn't be surprised that he hasn't shown up. I didn't exactly act like an inspiring mentor yesterday. I wait a good fifteen minutes, just in case he's late, and then call it. I consider practising penalties by myself, but I know that I need to put this right.

Coach made a good point last night and I'm embarrassed that I let my ego and personal vendettas overshadow the responsibilities of being a good captain and team player. I feel like I've somehow betrayed the sport, and if my dad knew about the way I acted, he wouldn't be proud of me at all. He has always taught me to be competitive and aggressive in my play on the pitch, but it's just as important to be respectful, too. Yesterday, I did not show good sportsmanship and I let my dad down. And that feels unbearable.

I head back to the changing room and get out of my football kit and back into my jeans and jumper, before walking in the direction of Arlo's college. It takes me a while to track him down, but after asking a few people lurking around his college bar, I find his room. At first I think there might be someone in there with him because I can hear muffled voices, but then I realise that it's a movie. There is, of course, a chance he's not watching it alone, but I've come all this way. I have to try.

Taking a deep breath, I knock on the door. The movie is paused and I step back, steeling myself. He opens the door and starts, his eyes widening in surprise.

'Hey,' I begin, offering a small smile.

He scowls at me. Using his foot to prop the door open, he folds his arms.

'What are you doing here?' he asks coldly.

'We were meant to have practice today.'

He clears his throat. 'Yeah, I don't think the whole private training sessions are working for me. So I'm out. Thanks, though, and good luck with everything.'

He goes to shut the door, but I put my hand out to stop it.

'Wait, Arlo, let me apologise,' I say hurriedly. 'I'm sorry about yesterday. I was out of order. I was cross about other things and I took it out on you, and I'm sorry. I was ... uh ... well, I was a shit.'

He snorts. 'Understatement.'

'I really am sorry,' I emphasise. 'I feel terrible about it. I totally get why you wouldn't want to train with me, but let me take you for a drink to apologise. Please?'

Looking at me carefully, he eventually lets out a heavy sigh and nods.

'All right. Let me get my jacket.'

I hold the door open while he grabs one from the top of the pile of clothes on his desk chair. Glancing at the screen of his laptop perched on top of his duvet, I notice that he was watching a black-and-white film, which seems like an odd choice.

He notices my expression and frowns.

'What?' he says, following my eyeline to his laptop.

'Nothing,' I say quickly. 'Ready?'

'Yeah, let's go.'

I decide to take him to a small speakeasy-vibe gin bar, an intimate upmarket place that won't be packed full of students or anyone we might know. I attempt small talk on the way there, but our conversation feels hollow and strained, so I give up, and we walk in silence. While he secures a table, I head to the bar to order our drinks, getting two gin and tonics and, glancing back at him sitting there scrolling through his phone, hastily adding a couple of tequilas to our order. Arlo Hudson annoys me enough without the advantage of sitting up on a high horse with me grovelling for his forgiveness – I'm going to need tequila to get through this in one piece.

When I return to our table, he looks amused as he watches me down the shot and then wash it back with two large gulps of my gin and tonic. The hint of an intrigued smile on his face gives me a flicker of hope that he doesn't hate me completely.

'Nervous?' he asks, ignoring his shot and taking a sip of his gin.

'No,' I automatically respond, then hesitate. 'A little.'

'I'm flattered. I didn't think you were the type of person who got nervous.'

'Why would you think that?'

'I've seen you play football.'

'I'm different when I'm on the pitch,' I explain. 'And anyway, everyone gets nervous sometimes.'

'But not when you play?'

I shrug. 'Not really. Actually, that's a lie. I get nervous just before play begins when I have to take penalties in an important match. Apart from those big moments, I guess I'm too engrossed in the sport to pay any attention to nerves.'

He smiles to himself. 'Brits and penalties. Never a good combination.'

'I think you'll find you're talking about the *English*,' I remind him. 'Scots don't have a complicated relationship with penalties.'

'My mistake.'

He takes another sip of his drink. I follow suit. I should say what I came here to say, but I can't bring myself to get to the awkward bit. Not yet. I take another large gulp.

'What were you watching tonight?' I ask breezily, placing my glass down.

'*The Big Sleep*,' he says, sitting back in his chair. 'You seen it?'

I shake my head.

'It's a classic,' he tells me. 'Humphrey Bogart and Lauren Bacall – lots of chemistry.'

'It's a romance?'

'A film noir,' he says, before looking thoughtful for a moment and adding, 'with a bit of romance thrown in.'

'I didn't have you down as a black-and-white film fan,' I admit.

He raises his eyebrows. 'Why? Do I not look arty and pretentious enough to be the kind of person who likes old movies?'

I can't help but laugh. 'Well ... yeah! Sounds stupid when you say it like that, though.'

'That's because it is stupid.' The corners of his lips twitch into a smile. 'My mom likes those movies, so we grew up watching them. I find them comforting when I feel homesick.'

'You get homesick?' I say, unable to hide my surprise at him being so openly vulnerable in front of me, his nemesis.

'Course,' he replies, unfazed. 'I'm a long way from home.'

I nod, taking another swig of gin. '*The Big Sleep*. I'll have to add that to my list.'

'I can give you some good recommendations,' he

says. 'Actually, I have a few classics to watch myself that I've never seen – I'm taking a film module and a big part of it is the Golden Age of Hollywood.'

'What are you studying?'

'English literature.'

'You're a *bookworm*?'

A knowing smile spreads across his face. 'Sadie, I'm finding it hard not to be insulted at how surprised you look every time you find out something new about me. It's like you can't get your head around the fact that I have other interests aside from soccer.'

'I'm sorry,' I say, blushing. 'I . . . I guess I just . . .'

'Had a certain impression of me?' he finishes.

'I'm sure you have a certain impression of me too,' I counter. 'And I'm sure it isn't a very flattering one. Which is very much deserved after yesterday.'

He doesn't say anything. I take another drink and then a deep breath. It's time to address the elephant in the room.

'Again, I'm so sorry, Arlo,' I blurt out. 'I promise you I'm not . . . I don't usually act like that. I wasn't myself. Please forgive me for being such a cocky little shit.'

He finally picks up his shot and downs it, wincing as he bites into the wedge of lemon after.

'All right,' he says, placing the lemon and empty glass down on the table. 'Why weren't you yourself?'

'Various reasons,' I answer vaguely.

'To do with Hayley and Dylan?' he guesses, sipping his gin and tonic. 'I heard that you and her used to date.'

'It was nothing,' I say with a wave of my hand.

He gives me a look. I sigh.

'Okay, it wasn't *nothing*,' I admit. 'It was a short-lived but intense fling. I liked her. Whatever. She's moved on.'

'Very openly,' he observes. 'Can't be easy for you and the team.'

'Like I keep reminding them, we were together for a few weeks. It isn't this big deal that everyone makes it out to be. We're perfectly capable of remaining professional about the whole thing.' I hesitate. 'I don't really get what she sees in Dylan Carson, though.'

'Dylan's all right.'

'Oh yeah, I forgot you were friends.'

He shrugs. 'We're not exactly close friends. He's fun to hang out with. Not sure he's captain material, though.'

'I'm not sure my team thinks I'm captain material after yesterday,' I remark glumly. 'Not my finest moment.'

'Hey, it happens. We all have our off days,' Arlo says. 'You're a brilliant captain.'

I blink at him in surprise. He glances at my expression and bursts out laughing.

'What? Shocked that I have the ability to be nice?' He chuckles. 'If you'd bothered to talk to me before tonight, you might have discovered that sooner.'

'I've talked to you,' I say defensively.

'Barely. You hold grudges – that much is obvious,' he comments. 'Ever since our first meeting at Osbournes, you've refused to give me the time of day. All because I pushed in front of you at the bar.'

'Ah!' I sit up in my seat. 'So you admit you pushed in.'

He grins at me. 'I'm starting to understand you a bit more, Sadie McGrath. Not only do you hold grudges, but you also have to win – whether it's on the pitch or off it.'

'Actually, my competitive spirit is usually contained to the perimeters of a football pitch,' I correct him. 'It's not like you did much to help me get over my grudge. You didn't seem overjoyed when Coach asked me to help train you, and then you made it very clear you didn't want to be there.'

'Because you made me feel so welcome,' he comments sarcastically.

I shift in my seat. 'It's not personal. I'm still not convinced it's the best use of my time, that's all. I need to focus on myself and being the best I can be.'

'Can I ask you something? I don't want you to take this the wrong way,' he begins, leaning forward on the table and looking at me curiously. 'Why are you so invested in this tournament? I get that you love soccer ... Sorry, football. But it's just university football, right? It's not serious.'

'It is to me,' I say, nodding. 'There's nothing more important to me than this.'

He tilts his head. 'Why?'

Sighing heavily, I get to my feet.

'Before we get into this, I'm going to get another drink,' I inform him. 'Same again?'

'Sure,' he says, looking surprised but smiling up at me. 'Throw in some more tequilas, too. I have a feeling we might need them.'

CHAPTER EIGHT

We slam the shot glasses down on the table and, while I grimace at the burning sensation in my throat that makes my eyes water, Arlo gets himself comfortable.

'Okay,' he begins, clasping his hands together, 'so why is there nothing more important to you than the BOB Championship? Wait, that doesn't sound right. What's it called?'

'The BUCS Championship,' I correct, chuckling at his mistake. 'It's the British Universities and Colleges Sport football competition.'

'That's the one.' He grins. 'Why is it such a big deal?'

'Because we've won it the last two years in a row, and if we win it for the third time, we'll be the first team in its history to do so. I'm captain this year and that's a big deal if I lead the team to that kind of victory.'

'Sure.' He hesitates. 'But that's not the main reason it's so important to you. There's something bigger going on.'

'You're right,' I admit, reaching for my gin. 'Scouts sometimes come to the finals.'

He raises his eyebrows. 'As in, football scouts looking for players to go pro.'

'Exactly.' I bite my lip. 'I know it's late to be noticed, but Coach Hendricks has talked to me about it and agreed that I might have a chance. It's happened for university players before, so, if I play well, it could happen for me.'

'Wow, okay, I get it now,' he says, looking impressed.

'I *need* to get scouted this year,' I sigh, swirling the ice in my glass. 'Otherwise it could be too late.'

'I get that most pro footballers are scouted earlier, but it happens later for people, too,' he says, looking down at his hands. 'There's still time.'

'Actually, that's not what I meant,' I reveal, the tequila encouraging me to be completely candid with him. He looks up with interest. 'I'm talking about it being too late for my dad.'

He frowns in confusion. 'Your dad?'

I nod slowly, taking a few sips of my drink before daring to say it out loud to a guy I barely know and whose company I usually can't stand. But there's something about the way he's looking at me – those intense brown eyes willing me to trust him.

'He's sick,' I say quietly. 'He has young-onset dementia. The condition progresses quickly and I want him to understand that I've been signed for pro football before things get so bad that his communication skills break down or he can't recognise who I am any more. Aside from family, football is everything to him – he used to play for Scotland – and I want him to be proud of me. I need him to know that I'm going to make it.'

His brow furrowed, Arlo nods. I'm sorry, Sadie,' he says simply. 'That must be ... When did you get his diagnosis?'

'A couple of years ago. That's when I took up football seriously,' I explain.

He stares at me, stunned. 'You only started playing two years ago? Seriously?'

'Technically, I've played my whole life, but not properly.

I never enjoyed it when I was young. Dad tried his best to get me into it. He was convinced I had the talent to play professionally, but I refused to do the training. If I'd listened to him, then by now I might have already been signed to a club.' I sigh. 'Hindsight is a wonderful thing.'

'Hang on, let me get my head round this,' Arlo says, after taking a few gulps of his drink. 'You're telling me that, at one point, you – football-obsessed Sadie McGrath – *didn't like football*?'

'It's more that I was scared of being bad at it,' I say, laughing at his reaction. 'My dad was such a big deal on our road and at school – everyone knew who he was, this local football legend, and whenever I played, I knew everyone was watching me, analysing everything I did to see if I was as good. I knew I wasn't, so I felt like I was letting my name down or something.'

'Okay, but then two years ago, you decided to go for it.'

'It was like Dad's diagnosis kicked me into gear,' I confess. 'I realised that I was hiding away from something because I was scared that I would lose. But how would I ever know if I would win or lose if I didn't even bother to try?'

'A classic age-old lesson,' he says with a grin.

'Exactly. At first, I started training for Dad, but pretty quickly I knew I was doing it for myself, too. The place I feel most at ease is the football pitch. I've been playing as much as possible the last couple of years, trying to make up for lost time. Mum wanted me to come to university and get a degree, but I know that I won't be happy having any other career. I want to be a pro footballer, and I want Dad to be there when I achieve that dream.'

'That makes sense.'

'Yesterday, I spoke to him on the phone and he didn't realise he was talking to me,' I continue, my voice wobbling and betraying my pain. I quickly down the rest of my drink. Suddenly all sense has gone and I'm on a mission to lose myself in the haziness of being drunk. 'Hayley and Dylan didn't help matters, but that's not what I was upset about. I was angry at the world, and sad about the disease my dad is suffering from, and worried about what's going to happen, and tormented by guilt that I'm not at home with him and Mum to help.' I take a deep breath, adding quietly,

'If we don't win this championship and I don't get scouted, then I'll have wasted all this time away from him for nothing.'

Arlo looks deep in thought for a moment, his forehead creasing. Then, he stands up abruptly and I wonder if I've scared him away by blurting out my life story. Blushing, I'm about to apologise, but he walks off before I can, heading straight to the bar. I'm surprised to witness him ordering another round of drinks, returning to our table with more shots.

'Here,' he says, handing me one and taking another for himself.

'I'm going to be on the floor soon if I have this,' I admit, my head feeling fuzzy.

'Trust me, you'll need it for what I'm about to tell you,' he says gruffly, knocking his back. He waits for me to follow suit. 'Thank you for talking to me about your dad. That can't have been easy.'

'I'm sorry if it was too much.'

'Please don't apologise,' he says sternly, holding up his hand. 'If anyone needs to say sorry, it's me for teasing you about how important football is to you.

I've been a pain in the ass. From now on, our private training sessions will be serious. I promise. I'm not going to waste a minute of your time.'

I smile at him. 'Thanks. I appreciate it.'

'And in return for you being honest with me, I would like to be honest with you.' He leans back, lifting his eyes to the ceiling. 'I don't like talking about this stuff, so I'm just going to put it out there quickly, okay?'

'Okay.'

He clears his throat. 'A few years ago, I got scouted to play soccer for a club. It was everything I'd always dreamed about. My dad left when I was little, and my mom raised me and my twin sister on her own – I knew that if I could make it as a professional footballer, I'd be able to provide for her and give back for all her hard work, everything she'd done for me and Tamy, my sister. They couldn't have been prouder of me. They were my biggest cheerleaders. Then, one night after a match ...'

He pauses, his throat bobbing as he swallows. He reaches forward for what's left of his gin and tonic, and drinks it, returning the glass to the mat on the table.

'One night, after a game, my mom was driving us home and we were in a crash,' he continues, his voice low and unsteady. 'A drunk driver speeding down the road swerved to avoid what turned out to be a black plastic bag and slammed into the side of us. I was in the back. Tamy was in the front passenger seat.' He looks down at his hands clasped in his lap. 'She died instantly.'

I inhale sharply, tears filling my eyes.

'After the crash, I couldn't play football for a while,' he says quietly. 'My leg was injured badly in the accident. It took a long time for me to get back on the pitch and return to fitness – by then, the club had lost interest in me. I wasn't what I'd been before and there wasn't any guarantee I ever would be with such a bad injury so young. More importantly, my heart wasn't in it any more. I couldn't . . . I couldn't stop seeing her on the sideline.'

'Arlo,' I whisper, unable to stop myself from reaching out to him. He looks up sharply as I take his hand. 'I'm so sorry.'

'Thank you,' he says, his eyes locked on mine.

Swallowing the lump in my throat, I give him his hand back.

'It's been a few years now and it doesn't get easier, but I guess you get better at coping with the loss. Tamy always wanted to come to England,' he tells me with a soft smile. 'Our cousin lives here – he moved to the UK a few years back – and she always wanted to visit him. So going to college over here seemed like a good idea. I thought a change of scenery would be good for me, you know? When I got a place at Durham, I tried to avoid football but ... it's hard to ignore it over here. People love it.'

I nod. 'The beautiful game.'

'It drew me right back in. Mom encouraged me to try out for the university team. She thinks there's still a career for me somewhere in soccer, god knows what, but she likes to remind me it's the *only* thing I'm good at.'

I chuckle. 'Your mum sounds great.'

'Yeah, she is,' he says affectionately. 'I keep telling her I'm only playing for a bit of fun, though. I don't want her getting her hopes up.'

'You thought it would be fun and then you met me, the bitch of a captain who treated you horribly.' I grimace, burying my face in my hands. 'I'm so sorry.'

I feel his warm fingers grip round my wrist as he lowers my hands so I'm forced to look at him properly.

'Actually, if anything, you sparked something up in me that I thought was gone for ever,' he says in a voice I haven't heard him use before. It's gentle, sincere and serious. 'Just one practice with you, and I was reminded how it could feel. You made me want to be good at football again. You made me want to *win*.'

I swallow, my breath becoming shaky and uneven as his eyes bore into mine. He hasn't moved his hand from my wrist and his touch is sending shivers down my spine.

'Arlo,' I say eventually, butterflies flitting around my stomach.

'Mm?'

'Would you ... like another drink?'

'Yes,' he says, a smile spreading across his face. 'I would.'

CHAPTER NINE

It's funny how one night can change your entire perspective on someone.

Before today, I was convinced that Arlo Hudson was a deeply irritating, self-centred, conceited, brash guy who couldn't take anything seriously, but now I realise that I got him wrong. He's so fun and easy to talk to that time slips by without me noticing and suddenly I notice we've been sitting in this bar chatting for hours and I'm really quite drunk.

'We should go,' I say, checking the time on my phone.

'Yeah, okay. Hey, before we go, let's swap numbers,' he suggests casually, holding his hand out so I can pass him my mobile, 'so that next time I miss a training session, you don't have to stalk me – you can message.'

'I did not stalk you,' I protest as he smiles to himself while typing in his number. 'And there better not be a next time. You promised that you'd take it seriously now.'

'That I did.'

Having saved his number, he calls his phone so he has mine, and then passes it back to me. He stands up, pulls on his jacket and holds out his hand. 'I'll walk you home,' he states, as though there's no alternative.

I slide my hand into his warm grasp, our fingers interlocking as he leads me through the bar. Against my better judgement, I get a rush of excitement at the idea that others are looking at us and thinking we're together, believing that someone like him might want to be with someone like me. Without thinking, I squeeze his hand and find him clasp mine tighter in response. The touch of his hand combined with the alcohol is making my head spin.

Thanking the bar staff as he passes them, he opens

the door to go outside, halting abruptly in the doorway as he realises it's raining.

'You bring an umbrella?' he asks, turning to me.

I shake my head. 'It's okay. I don't mind the rain.'

'Of course you don't,' he says with a sigh. 'You're Scottish.'

He lets go of my hand to shrug off his jacket and hold it above his head, stepping outside and gesturing for me to follow him.

'Get under here,' he instructs.

I do as he says, stepping out and sidling up close to him, wrapping one hand round his toned, muscular arm and using the other to help hold up my side of his makeshift rain cover. We start giggling as we hurry down the winding cobblestone streets back to Collingwood. He has to crouch down to my height to make the jacket hang evenly over our heads, which makes walking quickly together very challenging. At one point, I stumble and he catches me, his strong arm taking my weight, stopping me from falling. The rain gets heavier and we give up on trying to cover our heads with the jacket. He drapes it over his shoulder, joining me in running down the last length of road leading to the college, both of us shrieking with laughter, getting completely soaked.

As we reach the door, I turn to face him. He stands close, his chest heaving up and down as he catches his breath. He rakes a hand through his hair, rain droplets trailing down his cheeks, dripping off his sculpted jaw. I can't take my eyes off him.

'Thank you for walking me home,' I manage to say, my voice raspy, my body swaying towards him, betraying the sense of longing I suddenly feel to be close to him.

'Thank *you* for asking me out on a date.'

'I didn't ask you out on a date!'

'You came to my dorm room and asked me to go for a drink with you,' he says, a playful smile creeping across his lips. 'Sounds like a date to me.'

'Well, it wasn't,' I clarify. 'I simply wanted to apologise for the way I acted yesterday.'

'I don't know why you're embarrassed, Sadie. I think it's really sweet that you came all the way to my college to plead with me to go out with you.'

'You are so annoying,' I murmur, rolling my eyes. 'I didn't plead and it was *not* a date.'

'If you say so. Whatever it was, it was fun. We should do it again.'

'You'd be lucky.'

'Yes, I would,' he says in a low, husky voice.

My breath catches in my throat. I glance up to find him watching me intently. His eyes searching mine, he reaches out and brushes his thumb along my cheekbone, pushing back the strands of hair that have become plastered to my skin from the rain. I part my lips slightly. His breathing slows as my heart races, thudding so hard against my chest I wonder if he might be able to hear it over the roar of the rain.

Lifting my chin with his fingers, he dips his head and presses his lips against mine. I find myself kissing him back urgently, wrapping my arms round his neck, my fingers tangled through his hair. His hands move down to my waist, pulling me into him, and our kiss deepens.

A chorus of squeals in the distance interrupts us as a group of friends come round the corner down the road, laughing with each other as they race to get out of the rain. His hands still grasping my hips, he presses his forehead against mine as I smile up at him.

I bite my lip. 'Arlo?'

'Yes?' he growls.

'Do you want to walk me to my room?'

'*Yes.*'

I slide my hand down his arm and lock my fingers through his, turning to open the college door and leading him up the stairs to my bedroom. We don't bump into anyone – they're all either out or tucked away in their rooms. I'm grateful Jade is out with her course friends tonight, safe in the knowledge that we won't be disturbed and I won't have to explain how Arlo Hudson ended up in my room.

I can't quite believe it myself, but here we are.

When we reach my door, he waits for me to open it, standing close behind me, his hands running up and down my waist impatiently, his warm breath tickling my hair. I push through the door and he doesn't wait a moment longer, spinning me round to face him and letting the door slam behind him as he presses me up against the wall, his lips crushing against mine before I even have time to turn the light on.

My head reeling from the combination of alcohol and the musky scent of his cologne, I pull off my jacket, letting it drop to the floor in a heap. He gently tips my head back to kiss along my jawline and down the slope of my neck, his strong hands sliding down my waist to my hips and round to the small of my back. I arch against him and he lets out a groan, finding my lips again and kissing me harder.

In the darkness, I guide him towards my bed, my fingers fumbling for the switch on my bedside lamp as both of us refuse to break the kiss the entire time. The room is filled with a warm orange glow and I giggle as our legs knock against the side of the bed and he loses his balance, sitting himself down on the bed and reaching for my waist to pull me down to straddle him. I cup his face with my hands as I dip my head to kiss him again, this time slower and more gentle, threading my fingers through his hair as he holds me securely on top of him. As I break the kiss, we pause for a moment, my breath fast and shallow. He gazes at me, his throat bobbing.

Hit by a wave of wooziness, I close my eyes, steadying myself by placing my hands on his shoulders.

'Are you okay?' he says, his voice full of concern, his hands gripping me tighter.

'Yeah ... I just ... I need a moment.'

'You need some water. I'll get you some,' he offers, lifting me gently as though I weigh nothing at all and sliding me across his legs to sit on the edge of the bed.

'There's some bottled water under my desk,' I tell him, pressing my hand against my head, willing it to stop spinning.

He finds the six-pack I bought earlier today and I hear him unscrew the cap off one. With a gentle nudge, he offers it to me. I gratefully take it and start sipping.

'Trust you to have a pack of bottled water in your dorm room,' he says with a chuckle, sitting down next to me and reaching up to brush my hair away from my face, tucking it gently behind my ear. 'Very responsible captain-like behaviour.'

'I don't feel very responsible right now.' I grimace, taking another sip of water.

'You need me to get you anything?'

'No, I'm fine, just a bit embarrassed,' I admit quietly.

'Don't be! I'm feeling pretty tipsy myself.' He pauses, his brow furrowed. 'Probably a good idea to ... slow it down.'

I exhale, passing him my bottle of water. He takes a few glugs of it.

'I think I need to lie back,' I say, wincing as I accidentally look directly at the bright bulb of my bedside light.

'Here,' he says, moving so I can slump back onto my pillow. He lifts my legs up onto the bed.

'Arlo,' I say, grabbing his hand and holding it tight, 'can you do me a favour?'

'What do you need?'

I squint up at him. 'Will you stay?'

'Yeah,' he says softly. 'I'll stay.'

I shuffle back to make room for him and he lies down next to me, putting his arm out so I can rest my head on his shoulder and nuzzle into his neck. Holding me close, he turns out the light and kisses my forehead.

'Night, Arlo,' I whisper.

'Goodnight, Sadie,' he whispers back, his warm breath tickling my skin.

I remember him kissing my head again before I fall into a deep sleep.

When I wake up in the morning, my mouth dry, head pounding, he's gone.

CHAPTER TEN

'Hello! Sadie?' Jade nudges me sharply with her elbow. 'I need your help. What do you think I should do?'

'Wait, what was the question?' I ask apologetically.

'I knew you weren't listening.' She sighs, slowing her pace as we walk down the cobbled street towards North Bailey in the direction of my next lecture. She's agreed to accompany me as far as her favourite cafe so she can pick up her third coffee of the day. 'What is with you today? You are so distracted.'

'Sorry, I've got a bit of a headache, that's all,' I murmur.

'You want some ibuprofen? I have some in my bag,' she offers, fishing a pack out of her designer handbag and passing them to me. 'This morning I was in a world of pain, but those have definitely helped. You should have come out with us last night – you missed a good night. You could have joined us after your practice with Arlo.'

I haven't told Jade anything about last night. I'm so embarrassed, I can barely admit it to myself. At least I can rest assured that whatever time Arlo left, Jade didn't see him go, since she arrived back at our college this morning looking hungover and dishevelled, still wearing her dress from the night before and carrying her heels in her hands. I'd had to keep my own personal hangover under wraps, which hadn't been easy, and resisted the urge to complain out loud about the fact that I hadn't heard from Arlo at all today.

No note, no message, no nothing.

If it wasn't for my pounding headache and the smell of his cologne on my pillow this morning, I'd question whether last night had happened at all. Thank god I didn't sleep with him; it would have made his lack of contact even more mortifying.

'You were out with your coursemates – I didn't want to intrude,' I tell her, taking two painkillers and a large gulp of water.

'You know you're always welcome. How was it, by the way?'

'What?'

'Practice with Arlo.'

'Oh. Um. Fine.' I frown, the heat rising to my cheeks, keen to change the subject. 'What was it that you asked me before when I wasn't listening?'

'The guy I got with last night, do I message him or not?'

'If you like him, message him,' I say with a shrug.

'He doesn't go to university here, though. He lives in London and was visiting his mate. So what's the point in striking up a conversation? It's not like it can go anywhere.' She slides her sunglasses up her nose, even though it's a cold, blustery day threatening rain. 'He was hot, though, and very funny. Plus, the sex was incredible. Honestly, Sadie, if it wasn't for the fact that he was wearing flip-flops out to a club last night, I would have said he was my dream man.'

I laugh. 'Well, there has to be something wrong with him. A fondness for flip-flops doesn't seem like a dealbreaker to me.'

'I don't want to seem too keen.'

'You want my honest opinion? If you spend the night with someone, it's nice to message them the next day, even if it's not going anywhere,' I say, my heart sinking at my own sad state of affairs.

'You're right,' she says, nodding as we come to a stop outside the cafe. 'If things were the other way round and he had my number but I didn't have his, I'd appreciate a message.'

'There you go, then.'

She takes out her phone and looks up at me, panic-stricken. 'What do I say?'

'Say something like –' I begin, rolling my eyes and pretending to swoon as I swing open the door to the cafe – '"It was the most amazing night ever and all I can think about is you and your—" *Shit!* Sorry!'

I am so caught up in my own performance that I walk slap bang into someone as they come out of the cafe, causing them to spill their freshly bought coffee all over their shirt. When I look up into the eyes of the injured party, I freeze.

'Oh my god, Arlo!' I gasp, heat flooding my face.

He shakes the coffee off his hand, grimacing.

'Hey, Sadie,' he mutters, his brow furrowing as he examines the stain on his shirt.

'We were talking about Jade just then,' I blurt out hurriedly.

Wearing a quizzical expression, he glances up at me. 'Huh?'

'I was saying what *she* should text someone. I wasn't talking about ... uh ... Basically, she spent last night with a guy and I was dictating a message. A fake one. Obviously.'

He blinks at me. 'Okay? Cool. I didn't hear what you were saying, I was a little distracted by the hot coffee splashing at me.'

'Right. Shit. Sorry. I'll buy you a new one,' I stammer, running a hand through my hair.

'No, don't worry about it,' he says with a weak smile, stepping around me to leave.

'Please, I feel bad – are you sure you're okay?'

'I'm fine, promise,' he assures me with a wave of his hand. 'My shirt took the hit. I'll see you both around.'

'Bye, Arlo. See you at practice,' Jade says sweetly,

before rounding on me. 'Sadie! Why are you telling people so freely about my sex life?'

'Huh?' I say on autopilot, staring after him.

'You just told him about me spending the night with someone! I mean, I'm not ashamed or anything, but he didn't even ask.'

'Sorry, I ... I thought he may have overheard what I was saying and thought I was talking about ...' I trail off.

She raises her eyebrows at me. 'You were worried that he heard you saying something about having an amazing night and might be under the impression that you were talking about football practice with him? I know you've told me he's arrogant, but surely he's not that vain, Sadie.'

'You're right, yeah, stupid of me,' I say, looking down at my shoes. 'Sorry, Jade.'

'It's cool. I don't care.' She hesitates and then adds breezily, 'Maybe it will make him jealous and prompt him to ask me out.'

I snap my head up. 'What? You want to date Arlo?'

'Aha!' A sly smile spreading across her face, she

whips off her sunglasses to point them accusingly at me. 'I knew it! You have a thing for him.'

'No, I don't!'

'Yes, you do. You can protest all you like, but I can spot the sexual tension between you two a mile off. Not to mention the flash of jealousy I just witnessed when I even *hinted* towards the idea of Arlo Hudson dating someone else. You *looove* him.'

'Oh, shut up,' I huff, marching into the coffee shop as she follows me, giggling. 'I do *not* like Arlo Hudson.'

'I might believe you, Sadie McGrath, if it weren't for the fact that your cheeks are as red as that fabulously glossy hair of yours,' she teases, joining me at the back of the queue. 'If I were you, I wouldn't worry – I can tell he likes you, too.'

'Yeah, because he was *so* friendly towards me just now,' I scoff, crumpling internally at the crystal-clear shame and rejection. He barely acknowledged me, let alone the night we spent together.

'Please! Thanks to your private sessions, Arlo has clearly got the measure of you. He knows that he has to be patient and play the long game to win you over.

You're not just going to take one look at him and fall at his feet like his growing fanbase.'

'He has a fanbase?'

She grins at me. 'Why would you care if he did?'

'I *don't* care,' I insist, frowning as I pretend to study the menu on the blackboard behind the counter.

'In case it escaped your notice, he's not too bad to look at, plus he's got the whole sports angle going on. He's like the classic sexy jock in an American high-school movie, except he's not a dick.'

I snort. 'You sure about that?'

'I think you need to give him a chance,' she says haughtily. 'You never know, he might surprise you.'

'Or he may prove to be exactly the kind of person I think he is.' I reach the till and shoot the barista a warm smile. 'Two flat whites, please.'

'Did it ever occur to you that he might be intimidated by you?' Jade remarks as I pay and we move to the end of the counter to await our drinks. 'You can be a little scary when you're playing football. Don't get me wrong, as someone on your team, I'm pleased about that. But maybe you put him on edge and make him nervous – he probably says stupid stuff to impress you. You should cut him some slack when you talk to him.'

I sigh heavily. 'Jade, I do not make Arlo nervous. Trust me. And, for your information, yesterday I was perfectly nice to him and we … bonded. A little. But then, I see him today and he barely looks at me! You were there. You witnessed how he didn't say much and then escaped my company as quickly as humanly possible.'

'Bloody hell, Sadie, you spilt a hot drink over the guy and then shouted in his face about your best friend's sexual escapades,' she says with a laugh, staring at me in surprise. 'What did you expect him to say?'

'Nothing! Nothing,' I say, my cheeks flushing. 'Never mind.'

She watches me curiously. 'What did you bond over?'

'What?'

'You said you bonded in the training session yesterday,' she says. 'What did you talk about?'

'Nothing important,' I mutter. 'I thought we'd broken the ice, that's all. Just now, we seemed liked strangers.'

'Do you have his number? Message him,' she suggests. 'Apologise again for the coffee incident. Go on, why not? You said it to me: if you like him, message him.'

'I told you, I don't li—'

'Sadie,' she interrupts, holding up her hand, 'please let's not go through this again. I barely have the patience for this kind of back-and-forth bullshit when I'm feeling one hundred per cent, let alone when I'm hanging out my arse thanks to the five thousand sambucas I consumed last night.'

I sigh, reaching for my phone, secretly pleased to have a solid excuse to contact him.

'Fine. I'll message him to apologise about the coffee.'

'Good,' she says, satisfied, as she gratefully takes the two flat whites that appear on the counter for us. 'I bet you anything that he replies with something flirtatious.'

For once, Jade is wrong.

That night, I experience the crushing feeling of being right about Arlo Hudson. He doesn't reply with something flirtatious.

He doesn't reply at all.

CHAPTER ELEVEN

In an ideal world, I would be able to avoid Arlo altogether, but I know that we're going to be forced to see each other almost every day of the week thanks to our team practice being at the same time and, on top of that, our private sessions. Thankfully, during our first team training session after the tequila night, it becomes clear very quickly that neither of us has told anyone else about our spontaneous night together. Though the men's team isn't training with us today, they're on the pitch next to us, and no one makes any comments or acts any differently towards me. I know the football lads well enough to be sure that if they had any kind of inkling about what happened, there would be some kind of remark. There's no way Dylan Carson *wouldn't* take the opportunity to embarrass me.

Thankfully, Arlo has the class not to brag about shit like that.

Just not enough class to message me afterwards.

I purposefully avoid looking in the direction of their pitch as much as possible. At one point during a drill, I accidentally catch Arlo's eye and he straightens, his face lighting up as he smiles warmly at me. I scowl and look away. When I take a penalty at the end of practice, I hear him applaud me and call out, 'nice one', but I don't acknowledge him. I'm humiliated enough without him making it worse by giving me sympathy praise.

As Coach blows the whistle and instructs everyone to clear up the cones and get out of there, I'm surprised to hear my name called out by Dylan.

'Sadie!' he says, jogging up behind me as I bend down to scoop up the football from where I put it at the back of the goal. 'Hey.'

'Hi, Dylan,' I say, puzzled as the rest of the teams

filter away from the field and into the changing rooms. 'You all right?'

'Yeah, good. I'm great,' he says unconvincingly, peeling off his goalie gloves and turning to check everyone else has gone. 'I . . . uh . . . I wanted to talk to you about something, actually.'

'Okay. What's up?'

He sighs, tilting his head. 'I wanted your advice about Hayley.'

I blink at him. 'You . . . huh?'

'I don't know what to do!' he exclaims, throwing his hands up in exasperation. 'She is so hard to read! What is that about?'

'Are you . . . ? Is this a joke?' I ask, glancing around us nervously in case one of his dickhead friends is lurking about the goalposts filming us secretly. But no one is anywhere near us – the pitches have emptied and the only people left are Arlo, Coach Hendricks and Coach Nevile, who are chatting metres away.

'I'm being serious. You have to help me,' Dylan insists, looking at me pleadingly. 'I feel like I'm going out my mind. One minute she's all over me – the next she's not replying to my messages. She said she wanted to be exclusive, but then last night, she barely talks to me and is being all flirtatious with this guy at the bar.'

'Um, Dylan, I don't think I'm the person to—'

'You know her better than anyone,' he presses, his forehead creasing. 'I know it's weird to ask you this stuff, but you're over her, right? You two are, like, mates now.'

I clear my throat. 'Yeah. Course.'

'So, is that normal? Was she like this with you? Should I be worried? I don't want her to dump me out the blue like she did to you.'

Dear god, kill me now.

'We didn't really have the same relationship that you guys have,' I manage to say, wishing the field would open up beneath me and swallow me whole. 'We didn't talk about being exclusive or anything like that.'

'Yeah, but you were kind of together for a bit,' he points out impatiently. 'She told me that you two were pretty serious.'

'She said that?' I say, surprised.

He shrugs.

'Look, Dylan, from what I've seen, she really likes you,' I eventually say, realising that he's not going to leave me alone until I've given him some kind of answer. 'I'm sure you have nothing to worry about.'

'Yeah? Okay, cool,' he says, nodding in relief. 'It's weird. I haven't really been in this situation before. Usually, I do the dumping, so I don't really know what the warning signs are if it's coming my way, you know? That's why I thought I'd ask you about this kind of stuff.'

'How ... sweet,' I say through a fixed smile. 'Well, if you ever want any more advice on being dumped, you know where to find me.'

'Thanks, Sadie,' he says brightly, missing my sarcasm. 'See you later.'

As he turns and jogs away, I shake my head in disbelief. I'm still reeling from the conversation when I emerge from the changing room later, having showered and dressed. Jade had to rush off after practice, but I'm already looking forward to what she has to say when I tell her all about that conversation. I'm sure it will be entertaining.

Exiting the sports centre, I'm still smiling to myself as I think about Jade's reaction, when I notice a huddle of people hanging around outside. Arlo is standing there, surrounded by three girls and a guy, none of whom I recognise. All four of them are giggling at something he's said and one of the girls places a hand on his arm. Ducking my head, I march past them as quickly as possible.

As I turn the corner, Arlo rushes up from behind and falls into step with me.

'Hey, wait up,' he says apprehensively. 'How was your practice? You looked great today. I mean, your play. Not you. Wait. Not that you didn't look great. You obviously look great as well. Okay, that all came out wrong.' He laughs nervously. 'Anyway, I was waiting outside the centre to talk to you about the other day.'

'What about it?' I say, staring straight ahead without slowing down.

'I wanted to say sorry for not replying to your WhatsApp about the coffee spillage,' he explains, hurrying to keep up with me. 'It was nice of you to message and I feel bad for forgetting to reply.'

He can't have any idea of how his words sting. There I've been, checking my phone every few minutes, studying the blue ticks next to my message that show it's been read, agonising over the fact that we almost slept together and wondering what he's thinking . . .

And he simply forgot to reply.

I quickly realise that I have two options here: be pissed off at him and prove to both him and Jade that I have somehow developed actual feelings for him, which, judging from this conversation, will definitely not be reciprocated; or I can shake this off, forget anything ever happened and save us all the embarrassment.

The latter is the obvious choice.

'No problem at all,' I tell him. 'I didn't notice you hadn't replied, to be honest. I just wanted to say sorry again for ruining your shirt.'

'Actually, the stain came out in the wash, so the shirt is saved.'

'Thank goodness! That's a relief,' I say, a little too enthusiastically to be sincere.

'Yeah! Thank goodness,' he says, matching my tone.

We fall into silence as we walk side by side. I clear my throat.

'So, how was training today?' I ask chirpily. 'I couldn't help but notice you haven't taken on any of my advice from our private practice. You missed that second shot at goal because you lost control of the ball. You were busy showing off.'

I notice his shoulders visibly relax and the lines on his forehead evaporate as he strolls along next to me, shoving his hands in his pockets.

'I thought I played pretty well today,' he retaliates, breaking into a relieved smile.

'You were bang average. We have a lot of work to do in our session tomorrow.'

'I'll be sure to pay attention.'

'Don't be late.'

'I wouldn't dare.'

As I turn to break away towards Collingwood, I fight the urge to look back over my shoulder at him. This whole situation is so *mortifying*. I sigh, wishing I could turn back time.

If only I hadn't gone to his room and asked him out

for a drink. If only we hadn't drunk all that tequila. If only I'd said goodnight after he walked me home to my college and turned away from him.

If only I could stop thinking about the way he kissed me, every time I close my eyes.

CHAPTER TWELVE

I try my best to keep emotionally distanced from Arlo, but that turns out to be a lot harder than expected. During our private practice sessions, I do everything in my power to keep things as professional as possible and limit our conversation to football, but he's so easy-going and charming, I find myself unable to resist falling into the trap of chatting to him about personal stuff too. Nothing too heavy, like we touched upon in the bar, but we'll talk about the kind of day we've had, what nights out we're planning, how our respective teams are doing in the championships and how we felt during the matches.

I find myself looking forward to seeing him.

He never mentions what happened between us, so neither do I. We both act as though it never happened, although thanks to that night, it's safe to say we understand each other a little better – I've softened towards him and he's certainly making more of an effort in training. We seem to be enjoying the practice more than we did, anyway.

But no matter how hard I try to forget about it, there are moments when I find my mind drifting back to it, remembering the spine-tingling moment when he first kissed me outside the college, how he pushed me up against the wall in my bedroom and pressed his body against mine . . .

'Are you nervous?' he asks me one afternoon during practice, jolting me from my daydream about him.

'What?' I ask, passing the ball to him, flustered. 'Why would I be nervous?'

'Your game tomorrow afternoon against Northumbria,' he says, looking at me strangely as he stops the ball beneath his boot. 'We were just talking about it. You were saying they're a good team. Haven't they beaten you recently?'

'Oh, that. They beat us in a charity match, but we'll win tomorrow.'

He looks impressed. 'I like your confidence.'

'We're playing well at the moment, despite our little hiccup against Edinburgh.'

'Just one loss in an otherwise perfect season so far.'

'One loss too many.'

He snorts, adjusting his beanie, protecting his ears from the cold. 'You're difficult to please, McGrath. There's you with all your wins, and there's us with our numerous losses. I just hope I play better tomorrow than last week. That was embarrassing.'

'That's not true – you were playing so much stronger as a team,' I assure him. 'You and Michael seemed to be communicating really well. You got unlucky at the end.'

'We lost, Sadie. They scored in the last five minutes.'

'Like I said, your team got unlucky. And, out of everyone, you were playing the best by far. I hope this doesn't sound patronising, because I really don't mean it to, but I think these extra practice sessions are really helping both of us. You're playing brilliantly at the moment, as long as you keep focus. Tomorrow you'll win – I know it.'

He doesn't look convinced, flicking the ball up in the air and bouncing it on his knee. When it dribbles onto the grass, he puts his hands on his hips and bows his head.

'Are you okay?' I ask, frowning at him. He looks weighed down suddenly.

'Yeah, fine,' he assures me, before adding quietly, 'I wish the game wasn't tomorrow, that's all.'

'It's natural to feel nervous before a big match, but you'll be fine.'

'It's not—' He stops himself.

I watch him curiously, noting the flash of sadness that crosses his expression as he stares down at the grass.

'Arlo, what's wrong? Is it something else? What's bad about tomorrow?'

'Nothing,' he says with a weak smile. 'You're right. Pre-game nerves, that's all.'

'Are you sure? If you want to talk about anything, then—'

'I'm fine,' he says sharply.

'Okay. Well, Coach Hendricks suggested we practise striking under pressure today,' I inform him, 'but if it would make you feel better to work on something else, say.'

'No, that sounds good,' he says, collecting himself.

'You're going to start on the wing and shift towards the centre, taking control of the ball. I'll act as defender and run diagonally across the box to position myself next to you and try to force you away from this zone. You dribble round me to the available space and take your shot. Got it?'

He shrugs. 'Sounds easy enough.'

'Does it now?' I say, raising my eyebrows at him. 'In that case, let's make it a tad harder and throw in some time pressure. You have thirty seconds to break round me and take your shot.'

'I'll do it in ten,' he retorts with a mischievous grin.

'Now, that's the kind of confidence you need tomorrow,' I remind him, jogging over to the ball and dribbling it into position. 'Let's see what you've got.'

He moves away, while I take my place at the edge of

the box. Checking he's ready, I glance at the time on my watch and give him a nod. As he runs to take control of the ball, I race towards him. Watching me approach, a grin spreads across his face and he laughs, attempting to trick me with a dummy shot to throw me off balance.

But I'm ready for that kind of play and, blocking his path easily, I tackle the ball out from under him, kicking it away towards the halfway line. I triumphantly turn round to find him standing with his hands behind his head, grimacing.

'I'm warming up,' he claims, dropping his hands.

'Me too,' I counter, unable to stop a smile. 'Let's go again.'

He jogs past me to fetch the ball and I return to my starting position. Checking my watch to remind him of the time pressure, I give him the go-ahead and we begin the drill again, only for me to tackle him once more. He swears under his breath as I kick the ball clear of the box.

'You're not taking it seriously,' I accuse him. 'You're laughing when I run at you. Do you not think I'm a serious defender?'

'No, of course I do! I'm just ...' He shrugs, pressing his lips together in frustration.

'You're messing around. This isn't a joke, Arlo, so stop making light of the situation. Be serious for once. Don't see me as me. If it helps, I'm not seeing you as you. I'm seeing you as the total loser I'm going to steal the ball from and could do so in my sleep.'

He whistles through his teeth. 'Geez. Charming.'

'I'm anything but charming when I'm playing football, and neither should you be,' I say sternly. 'Go again, and this time get the ball round me and into the net. Or would you rather carry on as you are and let me embarrass you all afternoon?'

He clenches his jaw and takes a deep breath in.

'All right,' he says eventually. 'Let's go again.'

This time, as I run at him, he's not laughing. Wearing a determined expression, he looks focused as he dribbles the ball close to him, keeping it under control with the outside of his foot as he moves around me and takes a shot at goal. I spin round to watch it hit the post. He throws his head back and groans.

'That was brilliant!' I say, clapping him.

He scowls at the goal. 'I missed,' he mutters.

'Arlo, you took it round me before I even knew what was happening,' I remind him. 'You kept control under pressure and found the available space. You were skilled and decisive. Next time, you'll get it in the goal. Come on, back to the start.'

With a heavy sigh, he does as instructed. We do the drill three more times – the first time, he scores. The second, I manage to block him, pointing out the lack in concentration that seems to come hand in hand with his complacency. The third time, he dribbles round me, shoots and scores. It's beautiful play. I give him a high-five as he comes running over afterwards, beaming at me.

'Once more?' he suggests, spinning the ball round in his hands.

'Let's move on and practise corners.'

'You're scared of me now, then,' he teases. 'I've proven that I can beat you.'

I lift my chin defiantly. 'All right, one more go. I won't be nice this time.'

He arches his brow. 'Like you've been nice all the times before.'

146

Moving back again, I watch him eye up the goal, trying to read his expression as he works out what he's going to do. When the corners of his mouth curl into a secretive smile before he looks up at me and nods, I take a guess that he's going to try to trick me, probably with some kind of feint. As he touches the ball, I go for the attack, racing in to tackle him before he has the chance to dodge me. I succeed in stealing the ball and I hear him cry out in frustration as I dribble it away.

'In your face, Hudson!' I yell, giggling smugly.

Suddenly, I feel his arms wrap round my waist as he lifts me into the air, twirling me away from the ball and plonking me down again. Cackling with laughter, he runs after the ball, keeping it in play and turning it back round towards his goal.

'Come on – Ref!' I cry out, before sprinting after him.

Catching him up, I try to barge him out the way as I go for the tackle, touching the ball out of his control, but in the process falling over and taking Arlo with me. We land on our backs in the grass, both of us laughing, our legs entangled.

'You are a sore loser, Arlo Hudson,' I tell him, staring up at the sky.

'And you are annoyingly talented,' he says with a sigh, pushing himself up on his elbows and twisting round to look down on me, his face speckled with mud from the fall.

We lapse into silence, both of us breathing heavily. My stomach knots as I see his eyes flicker down to my lips. He reaches over to wipe a fleck of mud from my cheek. He begins to lower his head—

'We should practise corners,' I blurt out, moving away and scrambling to my feet.

He looks startled at first, but then nods, following suit and standing up.

'Yeah, sounds good,' he says, brushing himself down. 'I'll go get the ball.'

As he turns to jog away, I take a deep breath, trying to slow my heart rate. That was a close one. I may be reading into things, but I could have sworn he was thinking about kissing me. I can't let myself fall into that trap again.

CHAPTER THIRTEEN

Later that night, I can't stop thinking about Arlo. My skin burns when I think about how we almost kissed, and I can't shake the feeling that he wasn't telling me something in practice today. I keep thinking about how cagey and weird he was when I asked him why he was upset about the match tomorrow and I have no idea why that would be. I consider that maybe he has a bad association with Liverpool or something, since that's where he'll be playing, but then I remember that he said he wished 'the game wasn't tomorrow'. It isn't the place that's the issue. It's the date.

I scroll through his Instagram to look for clues, but even though he has an account, he hardly ever posts anything. Sitting up cross-legged on my bed, I open my laptop and type his name into Google. Loads of unrelated links come up, so I narrow my search, adding in 'San Francisco' and 'soccer' to see if that helps. I press return and the first article that comes up is about the car crash. Swallowing the lump in my throat, I move my mouse to click on it, waiting for the page to load.

I scan the article about how the twin sister of a 'local soccer star' tragically died in the crash and how Arlo sustained several serious injuries. The driver was a powerful businessman and aspiring politician. He got let off all charges. Glancing up at the headline once more, I notice the date of the article and suddenly everything makes sense. Tomorrow is the anniversary of his sister's death. Of course. Why else would he be so affected?

Shutting my laptop and slumping back on my pillows, I close my eyes. No wonder he looked torn about tomorrow's game. He must feel so many emotions, grappling with memories about the crash and how his life changed for ever, as well as the grief of losing his twin. Maybe he shouldn't play. He might want to have the day to himself.

Or maybe he wants to play. That way, he has something to distract him. I think about messaging him and start typing something, before quickly giving up and putting my phone away. If he'd wanted me to know, he would have said something when he had the chance. He obviously doesn't want to talk about it and I don't want to throw him off his game.

The next morning, I try to focus on preparing for the match that afternoon, but I can't stop thinking about Arlo and wondering how he is. I don't see him all day – while the women's first and second teams are playing at home, the men's teams are playing away.

'Are you okay, Captain?' Jade asks in the changing room before the match as she pulls on her shorts. 'You seem down today. Is everything all right with your dad?'

'Yeah, he's … the same. Sorry, I'm fine. I'm just thinking about our strategy,' I lie.

Noting her concerned expression, I plaster on a smile and remind myself that this match is important. We lost to this side recently in that charity match, and my team are going to be all too aware of that – their confidence may be fragile and it's my job as their captain to bolster their belief. We need to win these points. So, shaking Arlo out of my head, I jump to my feet and clap my hands, calling everyone together before we head out onto the pitch.

'Okay, people, gather round,' I say, scanning across their apprehensive expressions as we stand in a circle round the bench in the middle of the changing room. 'I know this one might not be easy, but we have the upper hand here.'

'Upper hand?' Hayley looks unconvinced, crossing her arms. 'They are a really strong team and they beat us, remember?'

'That's why we have the advantage,' I insist as she frowns back at me in confusion. 'They'll be heading out onto the pitch today thinking that they already have all the answers to beating us, but we've learnt from our mistakes and we'll be coming back at them ten times stronger. They won't know what's hit them.'

'Yes!' Jade says, clapping me on the back. 'Love that! Let's show them what we're made of, right, girls?'

As the team replies to her positively in chorus, looking a lot more pumped and excited than they did before our pep talk, I turn to Jade and give her a high-five. Hayley waits for people to start filing out the room before she comes over to me.

'Sorry for being so negative then, Sadie. I can always rely on you to bring me up whenever I begin to doubt myself,' she says, shooting a warm smile at me. 'You are exactly what captains should be.'

Swishing her ponytail over her shoulder, she brings up the rear of the team rushing out of the changing room. As Jade shoots me a warning look, I assure her I'm fine and the only thing I'm focused on is the match. But as I run out to the cheers of the home crowd, I feel a little disconcerted about the fact that if anything is distracting me today, it's not my ex making a flirtatious comment right before I head out to play.

It's Arlo Hudson.

We celebrate our win at one of the big student nights in town, meeting the team there after heading back to our respective colleges to get dressed up. The club has two levels, one of which is reserved for the Durham sports clubs on a Wednesday night so we can congregate there after our matches without worrying about booking a space for the teams. As I step into the roped-off area, I notice a few people look in my direction and I blush, pleased to know that the dark blue cut-out dress and towering block heels Jade encouraged me to wear are having the right kind of effect.

'Here you go, Captain,' Amy says passing me a glass of Prosecco. 'To toast yet another win.' She looks amazing in a fitted red minidress.

'Cheers!' Quinn shouts at the top of her lungs, prompting our whole team to clink their glasses together and give a loud cheer above the music. 'We will be the CHAMPIONS!'

'Let's not get ahead of ourselves,' I plead, but Quinn is too busy shimmying to the music to hear me.

'It's going to take one hell of a team to beat us, though – you have to admit that,' Amy says, beaming at me. 'Look at you today, Sadie. That penalty brought us over the winning line.'

'You were the one who scored twice today, Amy, not

me,' I remind her. 'My head was all over the place in the first half.'

'May I remind you two we are here to celebrate,' Jade cries, cupping my face in her hands and giving me a big kiss on the cheek. 'You can analyse your play all you like tomorrow, but tonight we dance!'

'Fine,' I say with a laugh, as she grabs the bottle from the ice bucket and tops up her glass. 'What about the boys? Do we know how they did?'

Amy grimaces. 'Hayley told me that Dylan messaged her. They lost one–nil. And did you hear about your American?'

'He's not *my* American,' I correct, my face growing hot at the insinuation. 'But what do you mean? Did something happen to him?'

'He fouled someone and swore at the ref, so got a yellow card. The other team got the free kick and went on to score,' she explains. 'Apparently he was in such a bad mood on the bus on the way home that he didn't speak to anyone.'

'Sounds like you were right about his fragile ego, Sadie,' Jade says, rolling her eyes.

'No, that's not—'

I'm interrupted by the lairy arrival of the men's team. They have clearly been busy drowning their sorrows somewhere else for pre-drinks. They're totally pissed and when Dylan goes over to Hayley to plant a slobbery kiss on her lips, she bats him away and says, 'Ew, Dylan! You *stink* of beer!'

When I can't see Arlo anywhere, I ask one of his teammates if they know where he is, trying hard not to recoil in disgust as he openly looks me up and down, his tongue flicking across his bottom lip. He finally reveals that Arlo is with them, but he is having a cigarette outside. I manage to slip away from the crowd when everyone is distracted by one of the lads picking up the ice bucket and pouring it over his head to a chorus of cheers.

Stepping out into the freezing cold night air, I see him standing with two girls who are offering him a lighter for the cigarette he's bummed off them. As he takes a drag, he looks up and notices me, his expression brightening.

'There she is! Sadie, get over here!' he calls out, his words slurring.

I approach him cautiously and, with the cigarette balanced between his lips, he throws his arms open and pulls me up against his warm, sweaty body.

'Congratulations for today,' he mutters, steadying himself as I pull away. He takes another drag and exhales a plume of smoke, before returning his attention to the girls and using the cigarette to gesture to me. 'Hey, do you know Sadie? Her team won today. Her team always wins, unlike ours. She is top of the Premier North League – isn't that awesome?'

The girls smile politely and say congratulations, their eyes darting between me and Arlo as they try to quickly work out what our relationship is. They are both tall and blonde, wearing flawless make-up and doused in perfume. One of them is wearing a low-cut silver minidress and the other is in a crop top and high-waisted leather trousers. They're intimidatingly glamorous and beautiful.

'Thanks,' I say to them meekly, before turning to look at Arlo in concern. 'Are you okay? I heard about what happened in the match.'

'I'm fine! I'm great. Everything is perfect,' he

says, taking another drag. He glances down at my dress and raises his eyebrows. 'Wow, Sadie. You look . . . wow.'

'We'll see you inside, Arlo,' one of the girls says, taking that as their cue to leave.

I should tell them that we're not together, but I stay silent as they waggle their fingers seductively at him and head back into the club. He watches them leave and then turns to me with a dopey grin on his face.

'They are something, aren't they?' He hesitates, his brow furrowing. 'Hey, can you remember their names?'

'You didn't introduce us,' I say curtly, before reaching out to grab his arm. 'Arlo, I want to make sure you're all right. It sounds like you had a tough day.'

'It's just a football match.' He sighs, lifting his eyes to the sky. 'It is not a big deal.'

'It *is* a big deal. You don't usually swear at referees.' I pause as he lifts the cigarette to his mouth, inhales deeply and turns his head away to blow the smoke out. I frown at him. 'I've also never seen you smoke before.'

'Maybe you don't know me all that well,' he challenges.

'I know you well enough to know you're not yourself today. If you want to talk—'

'Oh leave off, Captain McGrath,' he scoffs, waving his hand about, leaving a trail of smoke through the air. 'We're here to have *fun*. We're here to dance, to drink ... and to forget about our miserable lives for a few hours of silliness.'

'Arlo, I know what today is to you. I know ... it's your sister's anniversary.'

His smile vanishes. He gives me a cold, hard stare.

'I don't want to talk about that,' he snaps. 'It has nothing to do with anything.'

'It's okay if it affected how you played today,' I say hurriedly, the words spilling out before I can stop them. 'I don't want your confidence to be knocked because you had just one off-day when you were thinking about—'

'I wasn't thinking about anything other than the fucking match, okay, Sadie,' he hisses, glowering at me. 'Why are you talking about this? I said I didn't want to.'

'I know – I just thought you might need someone to—'

'You thought wrong,' he states plainly. 'I don't need you, okay?'

I swallow.

'I don't need you to check on me,' he continues, gesticulating wildly, 'I don't need you to look out for me, I don't need you to ruin tonight for me – I don't need *anything* from you of all people. Unlike you, I'm here to have fun.' He takes one last drag and then flicks the cigarette onto the ground, crushing it under his shoe. 'I'm going inside. Have a good night.'

Stung, I blink back the hot tears that threaten to spill. I remind myself that he's hurting and lashing out, and he'll probably apologise tomorrow. It's not personal.

I hope.

Promising myself I won't let him make me cry tonight, I head back into the club, joining the queue for the bathroom so I can check my make-up isn't smudged. With my head held up high, I weave my way back through the crowd and up to the sports teams' area, determined to have a good night and ignore Arlo Hudson until he's sober. For the night, I'll forget he exists.

But that's easier said than done. As I step back around the rope, a loud cheer goes up from the men's team. Arlo is standing in the middle of a group of them, his hands round the waist of the blonde in the leather trousers who we were talking to outside, his tongue halfway down her throat. There's another eruption of whoops and whistles as Arlo lifts her up so that her legs wrap round his waist, both of them apparently unfazed by unleashing such passion in the middle of a public place. I stare at them in horror, feeling like all the breath has been knocked out of my body.

That's when it hits me.

I finally accept that I've been lying to myself for a while now, and from the sympathetic look that Jade gives me after witnessing Arlo's spectacle herself, she knows too. No matter how much I try to deny it and protect myself from falling, it's no use. I've already toppled head first.

I like him.

CHAPTER FOURTEEN

By the time Christmas break comes around, I'm desperate to get out of Durham. Since my spat with Arlo at the nightclub, things have been weirder than ever between us. Just like when we spent the night together, neither of us has formally addressed what happened and it's been hanging uncomfortably between us during our private training practice. No matter how many times I tell myself that it wasn't personal, I can't help but feel hurt at how scathing he was towards me that night. How he implied that I was dampening his fun and how he told me point blank that he didn't need me. And then I think about him with that girl, her legs wrapped round his waist, his hands gripping her thighs as he supported her weight, his lips pressed against hers. How can I act normally around him with that vision stamped on my brain for evermore?

He's been acting as glum as I've felt, and the only time there was even a hint towards the events, the atmosphere immediately soured. It had been three days after that night and we were due to meet for one of our private training sessions. He turned up on time and I found he was barely able to look me in the eye.

'Hey,' he'd said gingerly, leaning into some stretches. 'How are you?'

'Fine, thanks. You?'

'A bit hungover.'

'You were out again last night.'

'And the night before,' he explained. 'Three nights in a row is not a good idea. Pretty stupid of me. None of them were that fun.'

'Really? You looked like you were having fun on Wednesday night to me,' I'd muttered, before tossing the football towards him. 'When you're ready, we'll get started.'

I'd gained a slice of satisfaction when he looked

pained and embarrassed at my remark, but that had been that. It didn't come up again.

Jade had made a point of telling me that when she'd been chatting to Hayley, Dylan and Quinn, she'd stealthily tried to get the lowdown on Arlo and the blonde from the club, and Dylan had brushed it off as a one-night thing.

'Apparently, Arlo was really embarrassed about it the next day when the lads were all teasing him,' she'd informed me eagerly one night in my room as I'd tried to focus on my coursework. 'He was asking if everyone had seen them together, and Dylan was like, duh, you were basically shagging on the dance floor.' She'd hesitated, her eyes twinkling at me. 'Do you want to know what I think?'

'Go ahead,' I'd said, examining my screen, having read the same sentence of a scholarly article on the social unrest and political disorder in medieval Europe four times without it going in.

'I think he was trying to work out if *you* had seen them together. Why would he care about anyone else seeing him with her?' Jade says.

'Maybe because he realised it was inappropriate to have someone straddling you in the middle of a club?' I'd offered, glancing up at her. 'Jade, drop it. He made his feelings for me clear. He doesn't care about me and he doesn't want me thinking there's anything between us. If he wants to get with random people on a night out, that's absolutely his prerogative. We're ... friends. To be honest, we're barely that.'

'You admitted that there was chemistry between you during your practice sessions,' she'd argued. 'You said that he opened up to you and you had some really good chats. He doesn't talk to anyone else like that, you know. Whenever I talk to him, he always keeps things light and makes jokes. He doesn't discuss serious stuff. But he feels like he can with you. That has to mean something. Plus, I always catch him looking at you.'

'That will only be because he's trying to improve his football, and he talks to me about serious stuff because he's forced to. There's only two of us on the pitch during our practice – it would be awkward if he didn't say anything.' I'd sighed, running a hand through my hair. 'There's nothing between us, Jade. It was a stupid crush and I'm going to move on from it, okay?'

She'd held up her hands, admitting defeat.

Gazing out the window on the train from Durham to Edinburgh, I'd pondered the necessity of our private practice sessions now. Maybe when I get back from Christmas, I'll ask Coach Hendricks if we could drop them. It has been helpful to have someone to practise with, but it's not like either of us can learn much from each other any more.

The last thing I want to do while I'm at home is worry about Arlo Hudson. He's far away in San Francisco for the holiday and I have to focus on my time with Dad and helping Mum; there's no room for anything else. It's hard to ignore the changes in Dad, even in the last few weeks. He's struggling more to articulate himself, every now and then finding it difficult to express what he wants to say.

I'm so grateful that we have football – when we're talking about that, he speaks fluently and passionately, like his normal self again, and when he goes in on himself, upset about what's happening to him, I can strike up a conversation about the Premier League or recent news about a team or manager, and he'll brighten, intrigued about my opinion and ready to give his.

I'm glad to be home, but I'm also exhausted by the flurry of emotions I struggle with here: the hurt of seeing my intelligent, brilliant father navigate speech, the hope each morning that he'll be on good form that day, and the guilt of watching my mum putting on a brave face, knowing that she has to cope with his decline by herself when I'm not here.

Dad's mood is lifted on Christmas day, when we visit my aunt and cousins who live nearby, and that night I feel a lot more positive than I have all week. Climbing into bed, I check my phone. My heart jolts when I see a WhatsApp waiting for me from Arlo. He's online now, too.

Arlo
Merry Christmas!
You should have seen my goal earlier

I created the space for the cross and

when it came, dodged the defender and

ran in for the attack

I thought early enough to create

that space

just like you're always telling me to do

You would have been proud!

How has your break been?

I stare at the message, a little taken aback by its friendliness. Maybe this is his attempt at an olive branch. Taking a deep breath, I start typing.

Sadie

Merry Christmas to you

Sounds like great play

Where are you playing?

You home in San Francisco?

Yeah, the break's been good

thanks

You?

I can see that he's typing back straight away and I hold my breath while I wait for his reply. I wish that just the sight of his name popping up on my phone screen didn't send the butterflies in my stomach into overdrive. It's those damn eyes of his.

Arlo
It's good, but I'm ready for uni to start again
How's Edinburgh? Busy or relaxing?

> **Sadie**
> It's been chilled, but I'm seeing some old school friends tomorrow night
> We're going out somewhere central

Arlo
I've heard Edinburgh is a good night out
You'll have to show me sometime

I inhale sharply, my heart somersaulting. What does he mean by *that*? I shouldn't read anything into it.

I. Should. Not. Read. Into. It.

I'm trying to work out what to reply, but he messages again before I can.

Arlo

You been playing much over Christmas?

Sadie

Not as much as I'd like

Just kicking around the ball in

our local park

I miss practice, will be good to

get back to it

Arlo

You're talking about our practice, right?

Are you trying to say you miss me?

You can admit it if you like

I won't make fun of you

Sadie

How generous

No, I was not saying I miss you

It's actually been nice to have

a break from having to listen to

you whinge about training

Arlo

Aw you're so sweet

I can always count on you to boost

my ego

Sadie

Any time

Arlo

Are your school friends as warm and

charming as you?

Or is central Edinburgh quaking in its

boots about the rabble invading tomorrow

night?

Sadie

I'm the nice one of the group

Arlo

So it's going to get rowdy, then

Sadie

It usually does with the
school lot
Things tend to get pretty wild

Arlo

Wild? How wild??
Are you trying to make me jealous,
McGrath?

WHAT THE?! I sit bolt upright, clutching my phone. Okay, maybe the previous message about him coming to Edinburgh could be taken as a friendly, breezy thing to say to be nice, but there is no way that this message isn't flirtatious, right? RIGHT?

Where is Jade when you need her?! As I start typing

a reply, the adrenaline pumping through my veins is making my fingers tremble. Bloody hell, a guy I like sends me one flirtatious message and it affects my ability to type.

I am pathetic.

> **Sadie**
> Why would I want to make you jealous, Hudson?

> **Arlo**
> You tell me

OH MY GOD. I'm trying not to hyperventilate.

I need to be smart here. Let's remember that this guy told me straight to my face that he didn't need me when I was trying to look out for him, and then he went and kissed the face off some other girl right in front of me. Since then, we've been awkward and weird around each other, so I should not allow him to make me go all weak at the knees just because we're having a bit of a flirty WhatsApp conversation, probably because he's bored. I should put my phone away now before I get sucked in. I should *definitely* ignore him.

Although.

Maybe things were awkward and weird between us recently because we both have feelings for each other. Jade did say that Dylan had reported Arlo feeling regretful about that night. Maybe he lashed out when I brought up his sister's anniversary and then kissed that girl because he was completely off his face and she was all over him.

I bite my lip as I see that he's typing again and decide to test the waters with my replies. If he has the confidence to be so flirtatious, there's no harm in me playing along.

Arlo
When are you back in Durham?

               Sadie
          Why would you like to know?

Arlo

I have my reasons

> **Sadie**
>
> Next week Jade and I are
> visiting Maya at home and then
> we're all going to head back
> together

Arlo

I'll be back in Durham next week too
Let me know when you're there

> **Sadie**
>
> Why? Because you've missed
> our training sessions so much?
> Who knew you were such a
> softie, Hudson?
> I'm touched

Arlo

I was actually going to suggest going for
a drink
But I also won't say no to you putting me
through my paces
Like you continue to promise

WHAT IS HAPPENING? I can't believe he just
said that! What is going on? He must have had a few
drinks; this can't be him being sober. What time is
it in San Francisco? It's the middle of the afternoon.
He must have had a boozy Christmas lunch. I'm
so flabbergasted, I stare at the message, my fingers
hovering over the keys as my brain frantically tries
to work out what on earth to reply to that. Once again
I'm saved by him jumping in before I can get back
to him.

Arlo

Like I say
Let me know when you're back xxx

I turn off my screen and put my phone on my bedside table. After a few seconds, I pick it back up again and double-check those last few messages. I peer at the three kisses, making sure I wasn't seeing things before. Sliding my phone back on the table, I stare at my bedroom ceiling and wonder how I'm going to fall asleep tonight. My heart is racing.

I'd been desperate to leave Durham. Now I can't wait to get back.

CHAPTER FIFTEEN

Maya has been going on about how we have to visit her for a night out in Newcastle since we met, and Jade and I promised her we'd do it this Christmas, making our way there the day before we're due back at university. It's only a short drive to Durham tomorrow and Maya's so excited that she's planned a bar crawl for us of her favourite spots. My night in Edinburgh with my school friends was fun but a lot tamer than I'd hoped as a few of them were too hungover from Christmas, so I'm looking forward to a big night out with the girls and have dressed up for the occasion in a fitted green bardot top, high-waisted black jeans, heeled boots and bright red lipstick.

'Wow,' Jade says, grinning at me as I emerge from the bathroom where I've been applying another layer of mascara. She hands me a glass of vodka Coke. 'Just so you know, if you don't pull tonight, it's because of your chat. It certainly won't be down to how you look.'

We start at a classy cocktail bar in the centre of town and catch up on our Christmas breaks, before heading to the next place, which is a little less posh and has a lot more atmosphere. When Maya comes back from the bar carrying a tray of shots, I groan but take it willingly, grateful for the amount of pizza I ate before we came out in the hope that it's lined my stomach. Maya and Jade can definitely drink me under the table and I'm going to need to pace myself.

'Who do you keep messaging, Maya?' Jade asks, as we link arms on exiting that bar to walk down to the next one.

'No one,' she replies coyly, putting her phone in her bag and smiling at her feet.

Jade gasps. 'Have you met someone? You better start talking or else I'm going to steal your phone when you're not looking and have a sneak peek at all those cheeky sexts you've been sending while you're out with your mates.'

'I have not been sexting!' Maya squeals, cackling with laughter. 'But I *may* have got with someone the other night and we *may* be messaging.'

'Who is she?' I ask eagerly. 'Do you like her?'

'She seems cool.' She hesitates. 'She's out tonight, actually.'

'WHERE?' Jade demands to know, bringing us all to a sudden stop. 'Near here?'

'Maybe.'

I share an excited look with Jade. 'In one of the bars on our crawl?'

Maya sighs, scrunching up her eyes. 'Maybe. But I *swear* that wasn't planned.'

'Oh my god – quick, let's get to the next place so we can sit down and you can tell us all about her,' Jade declares, dragging us forward again.

By the time we move on to the fourth spot, the three of us are tipsy and over-excited about bumping into this girl, Heather, although, as we walk into the bar where she is tonight, Maya gives Jade and me a strict lecture on how we're not to get carried away. They've only just met and it's not a big deal.

'I wonder if you'll get married in Newcastle,' Jade teases, receiving a playful punch on the arm by Maya while I giggle, holding open the door for them.

'You go sit down,' I say, gesturing to an empty booth in the corner. 'It's my round.'

It's not too long a wait to reach the front of the bar and, when I get there, I smile broadly at the staff rushing around pouring drinks, happy to wait my turn. I'm in a good mood tonight and nothing can affect that, so when I accidentally knock the elbow of the guy who comes to stand next to me, I turn to him to apologise, even though it's technically his fault for squeezing in there when he should have waited.

'Sorry, I didn't mean to— *Arlo?*' I splutter in disbelief.

His eyes widen in shock.

'Sadie!' he breathes, his whole body tensing next to me. 'What are you . . . ? What are you doing here?'

'I told you I was visiting Maya!'

He nods slowly. 'Oh, right. She's from Newcastle. That did not click in my brain.'

'What are *you* doing here?'

'I'm visiting my cousin. He lives here and we're out with a few of his mates.'

'Weird! I mean it's not weird that you're out with your cousin,' I explain quickly. 'It's just weird to bump into you out of the blue, here in Newcastle, when you've been in America and I've been home in Scotland. It's like ...'

'Fate?' he offers, his eyes gleaming as he smiles playfully at me. 'It's good to see you, Sadie. We should ...'

Placing a hand on my arm, he leans forward to give me a kiss on the cheek. My body tingles at his touch.

'So, what can I get you?' he continues as he straightens. 'And let's not go through the motions of arguing who's getting this round. Since we both know I'll be getting served first, you can tell me what you want and I'll save you the trouble of wasting your night waiting here to get their attention.'

I roll my eyes. 'That sounds like a challenge to me.'

'Everything sounds like a challenge to you.'

'Scared you'll lose this time?'

He baulks at the suggestion. 'The only thing I'm scared of is you getting your revenge for losing this bet on the football pitch. I can feel the pain from the tackle now.'

'So it's a bet, then.' I nod. 'What does the winner get?'

'Glory, pride and a well-earned smugness. And the loser has to buy a round of shots for both friendship groups out tonight.'

I arch my brow at him. 'How many people are you out with?'

'Four of us, including me. You?'

'Three.'

He holds out his hand. 'I'm in.'

I shake it. 'It's a deal.'

Neither of us wastes a moment, both leaning forward on the bar desperately trying to catch the eye of one of the staff. Thankfully, for my pride and my credit card, one of the guys working there finishes up an order, sees me and smiles, coming over to ask what he can get for me, leaving Arlo to groan into his hands. Once he's paid and loaded the drinks onto a tray, he picks it up and we turn from the bar, making our way to the corner booth.

'I have to say,' I begin, turning to flash him a triumphant smile, 'I do feel a lot of pride, glory and a general well-earned amount of smugness.'

'It wasn't a fair fight with you dressed like that,' he remarks. 'I didn't have a chance.'

My heart somersaults.

Jade and Maya squeal with excitement when they see Arlo, jumping to their feet to give him a hug, both of them as shocked as we were at the coincidence of being in the same place at the same time. He calls his cousin, Sam, over to meet us. Tall, dark and muscular, Sam proves good looks run in the family. Jade's eyes widen in joy as he approaches.

'Arlo's told me about you,' Sam says conspiratorially, when Arlo is distracted listening to Jade and Maya fill him in about Heather. 'He says it's down to you that he got back his spark on the football pitch. It means a lot to know that he's playing properly again and doing what he loves. Thank you for helping him.'

'I did nothing. It's all him,' I insist, stirring my drink with its straw, my cheeks growing hot. 'He's been helping me too.'

Sam looks surprised. 'From what I hear, you don't need any help.'

'You know, I didn't think that either,' I admit, chuckling. 'But Arlo has inspired me to be a bit more ... spontaneous with my play. I was all about strict strategy. Now, I think I need to go with the flow a bit more and not panic when things don't go to plan. I should have more faith in my gut instincts. It's hard, though, to not play it safe.'

'Head versus heart,' he says, glancing over at Arlo.

'Exactly.' I take a sip of my drink. 'So when did Arlo fly into Newcastle?'

He gives me a strange look. 'What do you mean?'

'Did he get back from San Francisco this morning? Or has he been here a couple of days?'

'He hasn't been home to America,' Sam tells me. 'He spent the first week of the break in Durham and then came here for Christmas. I had to force him not to spend it on his own. The only way I got him here was to promise him a five-a-side match with some of my friends. Thanks to him, our team won by a landslide, obviously.'

I blink at him. 'He ... was in Durham this whole time? On his own?'

Sam nods gravely. 'He's never liked this holiday. Too close to Tamy's anniversary. I think he feels her loss even more on Christmas Day, you know? His mum decided to visit some of her friends in Florida for Christmas – nice for her to have some fun, get away for a bit. She said he could join her, but Arlo decided he'd rather stay in the UK.'

At that moment, Arlo happens to glance over at us mid-chat with Maya and his smile falters on noticing my expression. He quickly excuses himself and makes his way over to me, while Jade takes the opportunity to sidle up to Sam and strike up conversation.

'Why didn't you tell me?' I ask Arlo quietly, when I reveal what Sam's just said.

Pressing his lips together, he gestures for me to follow him outside where we can talk properly. Leaning against the wall, he shoves his hands in his pockets and looks at me hopefully.

'You don't have a cigarette by any chance, do you?' he asks.

I give him a look. 'Have you ever seen me smoke?'

'I knew it was a long shot. It's only when I get stressed. I never used to smoke until after the accident and then ... it was a bit of an act of rebellion to take it up. I stopped after a while, but sometimes it helps to mellow my brain a bit.'

I shrug. 'You don't need to justify your actions to me, Arlo. You want me to ask someone if we can have one of theirs?'

He shakes his head, looking down at his feet. 'No, it's okay. I shouldn't anyway.' He takes a deep breath. 'I'm sorry for not telling you that I was in the UK this whole time. When you assumed I'd be in San Francisco, I thought it was easier to leave it rather than tell you the truth. I ... I didn't want you to feel sorry for me. I wanted to be on my own.'

'But why? If it's a hard time for you, you shouldn't be on your own.'

'I know,' he sighs. 'But, I don't want to bring everyone down and ruin celebrations, that's all. No one wants to be that guy. I don't know – it's easier to be sad about her on my own and then, when I'm with people, be easy and fun.'

'I can understand that. But it's also okay to be sad and real. Otherwise you'll never be able to let anyone in, and that's not a good thing.' I hesitate, adding quietly, 'People want to be there for you.'

He brings his eyes up to meet mine. 'People like you?'

'Well . . . yeah.'

I fold my arms self-consciously across my chest. He notices the goosebumps covering my skin and straightens.

'You must be freezing. We should go back in.'

'I'm fine.'

'My jacket is inside – you can have it,' he says, his forehead creased in concern. 'Let me go get it for you.'

'Arlo,' I say with a laugh, holding up my hand, 'I'm *fine*. We'll go back in now anyway, but, before we do, you should know that I'm here if you ever want to talk about your sister. We don't even have to talk, if you don't want to. We could just hang out and watch those old movies you like.'

He raises his eyebrows at me. 'Yeah? You'd be happy with a Humphrey Bogart classic?'

'Sure. Just don't hide away, hurting on your own. Okay?'

He nods, his lips curling into a smile. 'Got it. Thank you. I . . . It means a lot.' He holds his hand out, nodding to the door of the bar. 'Shall we?'

'Let's,' I say, taking his hand in mine and letting him lead the way back inside.

CHAPTER SIXTEEN

Boarding the coach to Nottingham for our away matches a week later, I can sense the nerves from both teams. Nottingham has a strong men's and women's team. The Nottingham men's first team is top of their league, while the women's training practice after Christmas did nothing to boost our confidence. My team was slower and sloppier, something Coach Hendricks put down to the break. I can only hope that the disastrous practice gave us the shock we needed to perform better today.

Taking a seat by the window, I spot Arlo climb on the coach and I sit up straight, hoping he'll notice and choose the free space next to me.

We had such a fun night in Newcastle, even though

nothing happened between us. Jade and Sam got on really well, and Maya found Heather, so Arlo and I were able to spend the majority of it in each other's company, chatting and laughing, completely at ease. The next day, Arlo messaged to ask if he could get a lift with us back to Durham and, while Maya drove and Jade slept in the front seat, Arlo and I sat in the back. I tried to fight the hangover and stay awake for the short journey, but ended up drifting off. When I woke up, I realised I'd fallen asleep on his shoulder, his cheek resting on the top of my head, our fingers interlaced.

As he makes his way down the aisle of the coach, he spots me and smiles, but chooses to carry on past, taking a seat next to one of his teammates. I try to hide my disappointment, quickly putting in my earphones and selecting a motivational playlist, drowning out the loud bickering coming from Hayley and Dylan at the back of the coach.

When Jade plonks herself next to me, she plucks one of my earphones out and asks, 'How long is this journey again? Tell me I don't have to listen to those two for more than an hour.'

'Try three hours,' I say, prompting her to groan loudly. 'That's why we're staying overnight in Nottingham.'

'Coach had better have booked a nice hotel,' she mutters grumpily. 'We'll need a bit of luxury after this match, I reckon. That dingy place he made us stay when we played away last time was the worst.'

'I wouldn't be expecting The Savoy, Jade.'

She sighs, sinking down in her seat and closing her eyes as the final few take their seats and we prepare to set off.

The journey goes smoothly and we arrive in Nottingham in good time, settling into their changing rooms and getting ourselves ready to go and warm up. As we emerge onto their playing fields, Coach Hendricks is waiting nearby and he waves me over, a stern look on his face.

'A word, McGrath,' he says in a low voice, leading me away from the others. He folds his arms. 'I wanted you to know that there's a scout watching today.'

I inhale sharply. 'Seriously?'

He nods towards a bearded man in a black softshell jacket, sitting on his own in the stand.

'Stay focused on the game. Don't be afraid to take risks,' Coach advises, watching me closely. 'You were a bit distracted this week in practice. Everything all right?'

My eyes flicker towards Arlo as he warms up with one of his teammates.

'Yeah, fine,' I assure him. 'It was just coming back from the break, that's all.'

'Break's over, McGrath,' he tells me, like I don't already know. 'This is serious. Impress this guy like I know you can do and we could be talking a potential club signing.'

I swallow, nodding.

'I think it's wise not to tell the others. I don't want to put them on edge,' he says. 'Better for them to simply focus on the game. Right, go help the lads warm up, would you? The men's league matches are scheduled first – then we'll go on.'

Jogging over to join the rest of my team as they stretch and do some warm-up drills, I try to ignore the crushing wave of nausea brought on by the knowledge that this could be a life-changing match for me. I don't feel ready.

I'm temporarily distracted from my own worries at the commotion caused by Coach Nevile telling Arlo she's benching him, reminding him of his behaviour at the last away match that landed him a yellow card.

'I was having a bad day!' he argues furiously, throwing his hands up. 'Come on, I don't need this punishment, Coach. I should be out there giving the team a chance at winning. You're making a bad decision!'

'You were told last term that this was the consequence, Hudson,' she responds unflinchingly. 'Question the decisions of your coach again and you won't see another match this term – got it?'

His jaw clenching, he backs away, shaking his head. I give him time to cool down and, once the match has started, make my way over to the end of the field where he's supposedly practising passes with another substitute, but he's kicking the ball way too forcefully and lacking any control.

'Are you all right?' I ask gingerly, taking over passing duties as his teammate runs to get some water. 'You know she doesn't actually want you *not* to play, right?'

'Then why doesn't she put me on?' he grumbles, glancing to the pitch where the score remains nil–nil. 'It's like she doesn't want us to win. They need me!'

'Yeah, and she's proving to you that you need them.'

He stops the ball and puts his hands on his hips.

'You think she's making some kind of point?'

'How do you think it makes the rest of your team feel, hearing you say that they need you to win?' I challenge him. 'Do you think that will make them play the best they can? Or do you think it will make them feel a bit shit and demotivated? And I'm guessing you're not feeling too great right now, either. You're frustrated and angry at yourself.'

He exhales, looking down at the ground.

'I'm not denying you're the star striker, but you're not the only member of the team,' I continue calmly. 'Punishing you for lashing out last term doubles up as a handy way for your coach to show you that they can get on just fine without you, while reminding you how much you enjoy playing alongside these guys. Two birds, one stone.'

He looks over at Coach Nevile as she stands on the

sideline yelling at her team to look alive, before he returns his attention to me.

'You think there's still a chance she'll bring me on to play today, then.'

'No doubt about it,' I state. 'But she needs a team player, not a solo star. Keep your attitude in check, support your teammates, and when you go on, trust them.' I smile wryly at him. 'In other words, don't hog the ball, Hudson.'

I'm satisfied to see he can't fight a smile.

His teammate returns and I leave them to it, joining Jade and Maya cheering our boys on at the edge of the pitch. When Coach Nevile substitutes Arlo on for the second half when it remains nil–nil, he runs on looking much more upbeat and motivated than before.

The ref blows the whistle and play begins, Coach Hendricks coming to stand next to me to observe them.

'Marked improvement in Hudson's play the last few weeks,' Coach comments, watching Arlo as he darts around the pitch, shaking off his defender. 'Coach Nevile and I have agreed that's largely down to you. Should things not work out with the scout, you should still be proud of yourself by the end of this season, McGrath.'

Nottingham score in the last ten minutes and my heart sinks for the boys, but Arlo doesn't seem to be all that affected. While Dylan chucks the ball forward from the goal, swearing at the defenders, Arlo shouts out words of encouragement, and I proudly watch as in the following few minutes, he gives an assist to Michael, who goes on to score, sending our team and the away fans in the stand into a frenzy. The final whistle blows and our side cheers the draw, a fantastic result against the reigning champions. I clap my hands until they sting, beaming at Arlo as he celebrates with Michael.

'Are you ready?' Coach says in a low voice, leaning towards me. 'It's your time now.'

Taking a deep breath, I shake my hands out, my fingers tingling with nerves.

This could be it.

CHAPTER SEVENTEEN

There's a knock on the door to the changing room. On receiving no answer, Arlo cautiously opens it and calls out my name, his voice echoing through the empty space.

'Sadie? You in here?' He spots me sitting alone on the bench. 'Is anyone else in here or am I okay to come in?'

'It's just me.'

He steps in cautiously, letting the door shut behind him. He comes to sit next to me.

'I've been waiting for you to come out,' he says gently, leaning back against the row of lockers behind us. 'Jade said you were the last one in here and you'd be out in a minute. That was –' he checks his watch – 'ten minutes ago. I was worried something had happened to you. You'd got yourself stuck in a locker or something.'

I manage a weak smile.

He frowns in confusion. 'Usually, when someone wins a match, there's a big celebration afterwards.'

'I don't really feel like celebrating,' I admit quietly.

'But you played so well today!'

'Not that well. I could have scored another goal if I hadn't hesitated when Alisha intercepted the ball and sent it up to me. I was taken by surprise and I messed it up because I didn't have a plan. I missed my shot.'

'What?' He looks at me wide-eyed. 'What are you talking about?! Sadie, you *won*.'

I shrug.

'Word is there's going to be a big night out tonight,' he says, nudging me with his elbow. 'I think Dylan is leading the charge, which means we'll probably all end up somewhere disgusting. Let's hope he'll listen to Hayley and pick somewhere where the alcohol doesn't taste like petrol.' He pauses, watching me curiously. 'Do you mind me asking why you don't feel like celebrating? I don't want to pry.'

'It's okay.' I hesitate. 'It sounds pathetic.'

'Try me.'

I lean back next to him and sigh. 'There was a scout watching us today.'

He starts. 'Really? Who?'

'He was in the stand. Coach Hendricks pointed him out to me before the match. I thought that . . .' I trail off, shaking my head. 'Anyway, he's gone now.'

'The scout?'

'Yeah.'

'Did he talk to you before he left?'

'No.'

'Ah.' Arlo nods in understanding. 'Sorry, Sadie.'

'It was stupid of me to get my hopes up. But when I scored that second goal, I glanced over at the scout and he was clapping . . . I don't know, for a minute I let myself believe that after the match, I might have a life-changing conversation. I pictured telling my dad. I saw his face, his excitement and pride.' I pause, lowering my head and blinking back tears. 'It was stupid of me.'

'Hey, it wasn't stupid,' Arlo says gently, swivelling to face me properly. He reaches out to take my hand in his, squeezing it. 'You had every right to get your hopes up. You played brilliantly.'

'I played too safe. I didn't stand out.' I swallow the lump in my throat. 'I wasn't enough. Maybe I never will be.'

'Sadie, look at me,' he insists, waiting until I've forced myself to bring my eyes up to meet his. 'You are one of the most beautiful players I've ever seen on a pitch. You were born to do this. You hear me? You are *going to make it.*'

'But the scout—'

'That scout is clearly shit at his job,' Arlo cuts in. 'He's missed the opportunity to identify one of the future stars of women's football. That's his problem and he'll have to live with that haunting regret. Forget him. There will be other scouts and more opportunities. This wasn't it, but that doesn't mean it's not coming for you.'

I sniff, unable to stop a tear rolling down my cheek. 'You really mean that?'

'Yeah, I do,' he says with a smile, letting go of my hand to wipe the tear away with his thumb. 'You're one of a kind, Sadie McGrath. One day, when you've forgotten who I am, I'll get to brag about the fact that you were once my mentor. "If only I had listened to her," I'll be saying down the pub.'

'You're admitting that you don't listen to me, then,' I point out, chuckling.

'Actually, you made a lot of sense today. Without you, we wouldn't have scored.' He jumps to his feet enthusiastically. 'Which is why I would like to take you to dinner tonight, to say thank you for your little pep talk. You managed to tell me to stop being a dick but in much nicer terms. Very impressive.'

'I am proud of that.'

'We will also be celebrating your big win tonight. No scout is allowed to take that away from you and make you feel anything less than a winner. I've been recommended a great Tex-Mex restaurant and, if you ask me, you deserve to be toasted with tequila.'

I wince. 'Ugh! Please no tequila. Nothing ever good comes from drinking it.'

'Not sure I agree with you there,' he murmurs, before grinning at me. 'Fine, tacos but no tequila. That's my offer. Take it or leave it. Preferably take it.'

He holds out his hand. I stare at it warily.

'Unless,' he continues, tilting his head, 'you'd rather go for dinner in the place that Dylan chooses. I believe his mantra is, "Who needs tables when you have arcade video games?" I'm sure it will be a very classy joint.'

'Tacos and no tequila, you say?' I laugh, grabbing his hand in mine and getting to my feet. 'Sounds perfect.'

*

We head back to the hotel first to get ready and I tell Jade what's going on the moment I step inside our room. She gasps and pelts out the room, knocking on Amy and Maya's door and forcing them to come to our room so she can repeat what I've told her. When the three of them start squealing with excitement, I beg them to CALM DOWN because we're going for a quick bite to eat and it doesn't mean anything.

'Tacos are sexy,' Maya claims, rummaging through my bag to help me pick what to wear.

'Are they?' Amy grimaces. 'They're quite a messy food.'

'Amy's right,' Jade agrees, flinging some clothes out on the bed from her case for me to choose from – trust

Jade to have brought a wheelie full of options for one night out. 'You have to make sure you eat them neatly, Sadie. This is most definitely a date.'

'It is not a date,' I croak, my throat tightening. 'Is it?'

Maya nods slowly. 'He waited for you outside the changing room to ask you for dinner *alone* before you meet back up with all your friends. I think we have to concede that it is, indeed, a date.'

'Fuck.' I exhale, slumping onto the bed and running a hand through my hair. 'I'm going on a date.'

'With the hottest guy in football,' Amy squeaks, clapping her hands.

'Scrap that. The hottest guy in the university,' Jade corrects.

'Way to make me feel less nervous, guys,' I mutter.

'What about this pairing?' Maya asks, holding up one of Jade's miniskirts and a sequin top. 'Too much?'

'Too much for a taco restaurant, yes,' Jade states, while I nod in agreement. 'Although put that outfit aside for me. I'm going sexy tonight.'

'You go sexy every night,' Maya tells her, blowing her a kiss.

'Oh, you.' Jade grins. 'Sadie, what do you feel good in? Tonight is about confidence.'

I exhale, trying to think. A memory pops into my brain and I sit up straight.

'You know when we bumped into him in Newcastle? He made a nice comment about what I was wearing,' I recall excitedly. 'We were jostling to get served first at the bar and he said he didn't have a chance with me in that outfit.'

'That off-the-shoulder bardot top,' Jade says, clicking her fingers. 'Shows off your sexy collarbones. Such a flattering style. Did you bring it?'

Amy fishes it from my bag. 'Here it is!'

'I'm thinking that top with these,' Jade says, chucking her faux-leather leggings at me. She smiles smugly. 'He'll keel over.'

Having brought some speakers and apparently too excited to care about other hotel residents, Jade puts on a playlist of all her favourites. Beyoncé's vocals fill the room, prompting Maya and Jade to start dancing on the bed, while Amy does her make-up at the dressing-table mirror. Smiling, I go into the bathroom to do my make-up as quickly as possible before putting on the agreed outfit. When I come out of the bathroom so they can check the finalised look, there are further squeals.

'I told you!' Jade cries above the music. 'He will *die*.'

'If *you* dressed like *that* doesn't make him see sense and snap you up officially before anyone else can, then he is not The One,' Maya tells me firmly. 'What shoes are we thinking?'

'Ankle boots? Or high heels?' Amy asks, holding up both options.

'Or she could go flats to make it more casual,' Maya points out.

'Boots!' Jade exclaims. 'No. Wait. Heels. No. Boots.'

'Maybe flats,' Amy says, tilting her head.

'I think heels,' Maya asserts, before frowning. 'Actually, maybe boots?'

'Okay, you are all confusing me.' I sigh, putting my hands on my hips. 'I need someone to make a decision!'

'So this is where the party is! Can we get ready in here too?' Quinn announces, coming into the room followed by Hayley. She gasps at the sight of me. 'Wow, Sadie. *Nice.*'

'She's going on a date with Arlo,' Jade says with a giggle.

'It's not *definitely* a date,' I say, blushing and avoiding looking at Hayley, whose eyes are unashamedly trailing from my head to my feet. 'We're going for dinner before meeting up with you lot later. He wants to thank me for the extra practice sessions.'

'Sounds like a date to me!' Quinn grins. 'You look hot. What shoes are you wearing?'

'Actually, that's what we were trying to work out,' I admit, as Amy brandishes the options. 'Which do you think will go best?'

Quinn looks uncertain. 'Hmm. Not sure. Hayley, you're good at stuff like this. What do you think?'

Jade and Maya share a look. We wait in silence as Hayley studies me.

'It depends,' she says eventually, jutting out her chin. 'Do you *want* this to be a date, Sadie?'

'Yeah,' I answer truthfully. 'I do.'

'Then you should wear the high heels. He won't be able to resist,' she says quietly, giving me a sad smile. 'Trust me.'

CHAPTER EIGHTEEN

Arlo Hudson might just have the best laugh in the world. If he finds something a little bit funny, he gives this sexy secretive smile and chuckles softly, but if something is truly hilarious, then he throws his head back, a huge goofy grin transforming his handsome face, and gives a properly infectious belly laugh. The kind of laugh that brightens your day. A laugh that makes a warmth tingle through my entire body. It's so wonderful, it makes me want to make him laugh like that for ever.

He's currently doing that exact laugh because I've told him about the time a hawk chased me around Edinburgh Castle.

'This can't be a true story,' he says between wheezes, looking at me wide-eyed across our little table in the Tex-Mex restaurant.

It's a great place, intimate and fun with really friendly waiters, and the food is delicious. The heavy weight of disappointment I'd felt at being ignored by the scout earlier today has gradually faded away, and the relaxed vibe of the restaurant has helped to make me feel more at ease, despite my formal acknowledgement to my friends that this is, in fact, a date. He's dressed nicely for the evening too, in chinos and a navy blue shirt with the sleeves rolled up to show off his toned forearms. Earlier, when the doors of the lift opened into the hotel reception, he was there waiting and did a double take when he looked up from his phone to see me walking towards him. His eyes widening, his lips had parted slightly and he'd swallowed.

I'm not sure I'd ever seen him look that nervous before.

It was deeply satisfying.

'You're telling me a hawk literally chased you around the outside of the castle?' he checks, slapping his hand down on the table when I nod. 'How is that even possible? Do hawks just hang around castles in this country, trained to chase young maidens who they may deem as threatening?'

'There happened to be a guy demonstrating his birds of prey the day we went there on a school trip,' I explain, bemused by his enraptured expression. 'The hawk decided to have it in for me and he chased me around the big space right outside the castle entrance. When the handler finally managed to get him under control, he said he thought it was because the bird either really liked my red hair or it was somehow offended by it.'

'Your hair offended a *hawk*?' he says in disbelief.

'I prefer to believe that he was admiring it.'

'Now *that* I can understand,' Arlo says with a nod, still chuckling. 'Maybe it reminded him of a nice red velvet cushion upon which a regal bird might perch.'

'Ah, that's nice. What every girl wants to hear: that her hair is like a cushion.'

'A *regal* one,' he emphasises.

'An important distinction,' I say with a grin, reaching

for my margarita. We'd both stuck to soft drinks for the meal, but I'd felt the need for a cocktail before we went on to meet everyone else, and he'd ordered a Corona.

'It must have been cool to grow up in a city with a castle on your doorstep,' he muses. 'I'd really love to visit Edinburgh sometime. Maybe this summer, when the Fringe Festival is on.'

'You won't be back home in America for the summer?'

He shrugs. 'I'm not sure. I guess so, but I could always fly back to the UK early before term starts and visit Scotland. Would you put me up?'

I snort. 'I don't think so.'

'Why not?' he asks, arching his brow. 'You don't want me to visit your beautiful hometown? You embarrassed of me, McGrath? Is it the American thing? Because I can do accents. You say the word and I can be a different nationality entirely. Are the Scots fans of the Irish? Because I've got the Dublin accent down.'

I roll my eyes. 'You're more than welcome in Scotland, no matter what your accent, but you've

211

forgotten that I live with my parents, so unless you'd want to stay with them—'

'Why not?' he says, tilting his head at me. 'I'd love to meet your parents.'

I blink at him. 'You ... huh?'

'It would be fun!' he insists, his eyes twinkling. 'I can hear all about how adorable you were as a child and the feisty nightmare you became as a teenager – you had a rebellious phase, right? You must have done. I hope they have pictures.'

'Two can play at this game, Arlo. There's nothing stopping me from boarding a plane to San Francisco and badgering your mum for childhood tales.'

'Go ahead, I have nothing to hide. I can confidently tell you that I looked very cool with purple hair,' he says, shooting me a mischievous smile.

I gawp at him. 'You had purple hair?'

'And I used to wear a bright green bandana round my head at the time,' he reveals. 'I was in a punk rock band. Sadly, I had to quit the band to devote my time to sport.'

'Music's loss was football's gain.'

'I'll have you know I'm a natural musician,' he claims, taking a swig of his beer.

I smirk into my drink. 'Sure.'

'I am. People would come for miles just to watch me up there on stage.'

'Is that so? Tell you what, you can prove it on the dance floor later,' I tease. 'A natural musician is sure to have good rhythm. We'll see then if you're speaking the truth.'

'Fine by me.' He shrugs. 'What about you? Will I have the pleasure of seeing you storm up the dance floor this evening?'

'Doubtful. It takes a lot to get me dancing.'

He lowers his drink slowly. 'That sounds like a challenge, McGrath.'

'Everything sounds like a challenge to you, Hudson,' I say with a knowing smile, echoing his exact words to me in Newcastle. 'I was talking about alcohol, Arlo. Considering I've only had one margarita tonight, I won't be dancing any time soon.'

'I bet I can get you up on the dance floor having the time of your life, without any more than that one drink,' he says, nodding to the glass in my hand.

'The time of my life, eh?' I repeat, raising my eyebrows. 'That's ballsy.'

'I'm confident in my abilities,' he states.

'All right, then, go ahead and give it a try. But if I have a terrible time, then you owe me another margarita,' I tell him playfully. 'What do you want if you win and I have the "time of my life"?'

He leans forward on the table, lowering his voice so only I can hear.

'If I'm dancing with you and you're having the time of your life,' he says, his eyes flashing dangerously at me, 'then I'll already be winning.'

CHAPTER NINETEEN

I don't like it when Arlo wins, but tonight I'll give it to him.

When we left the restaurant, he was telling me an anecdote about one of his lectures as we walked to the club where the others were, and he took my hand in his, as though it was completely natural. As though we were together. It was exhilarating.

A loud cheer went up from the two teams as we arrived and, while I'm sure my cheeks have flushed bright red, Arlo didn't seem to care a bit, greeting our friends cheerily before turning his attention back to me and leading me straight onto the dance floor.

'Wait, don't you want a drink?' Jade had cried out over the thumping bass.

'Not before she's had the time of her life,' he'd called back, much to her confusion.

Under the prying eyes of our friends, he guides me through the crowded dance floor, weaving a path through all the zealous clubbers to the other side of the room where they won't be able to see us from their booth, no matter how much they crane their necks. At first, he goes down the comedy route, spinning round and making me laugh with some outlandish dance moves and impressive intricate footwork. Even though he's joking around, I can tell he's genuinely a good dancer.

'Having fun?' he asks, leaning forward to speak in my ear. He smiles when I nod. 'The challenge was to get *you* dancing, though.'

He steps closer and runs his fingers along the underside of my arms down to my wrists, lifting them up onto his shoulders, my hands resting at the nape of his neck. His hands grip the sides of my hips, pulling me towards him and pressing my body against his. My heart hammers frenziedly against my chest, the people and noise around us fading into a blur as he dips his head to mine and I look at up him breathlessly, our eyes locking. He moves us side to side, swaying to the beat of the music and my hands gradually slip down his broad, muscled shoulders to press against his chest, gripping his shirt tightly. My face flushes with heat and my entire body tingles with the thrill of this moment.

Lowering his head even more to nudge my nose with his, he waits for me to get the hint and lift my chin so he can brush his lips dangerously against mine, but refuses to kiss me yet. Cupping my face with his right hand, his eyes flicker down to my throat and he gives a satisfied smile when he sees me swallow nervously. Brushing my hair back behind my ear, he leans in to talk to me above the music, his breath hot against my ear, his musky, woody scent sending a shiver down my spine.

'Am I winning, Sadie?'

My head is spinning too much for words. All I can do is nod.

He's not smiling any more; he's looking at me with such an intense gaze that I feel completely powerless, overwhelmed and scared. Scared because I want him so much, I know that I can't hide it. His eyes are boring into mine, searching for every nuance in my expression, leaving me defenceless and vulnerable.

We're interrupted by Dylan, who appears from nowhere and throws his arms round Arlo, chanting some drunken nonsense at him about their win, while Arlo's eyes remain locked on mine. I'm grateful for the disruption to our bubble, breaking into a breezy smile as I look round for Jade, who is weaving her way towards us. She's dragging Michael behind her, who has her lipstick smeared around his mouth. He's looking at her as though he's won the lottery. It's not long until Hayley, Maya and Quinn join us with others from the boys' team, and Arlo and I are naturally separated as the group grows in number.

I play along for a bit, dancing and laughing with the girls, before ducking out and going to join Amy and the rest of our team back in the booth. I'm surprised to find Arlo has followed me, wrapping his arm round me from behind as I reach the booth and asking what I'd like to drink. He heads to the bar, while I slide in next to Amy.

By the time he gets back, he finds the spot next to me taken by one his midfielders, Jacob, who is drunkenly telling me how talented he thinks I am, leaning in close so I can hear him, one hand pressed on my arm. I try not to look too pleased at Arlo's expression when he sees us, his jaw twitching and his eyes narrowing at his friend. I politely excuse myself from the conversation and stand up to make my way to Arlo, taking the drink from him gratefully so there's no mistaking my intentions for the night. His shoulders instantly relax and he leans in to kiss me on the cheek.

'Jacob looked a bit too close for comfort there,' he remarks, throwing a shady look at his teammate, who cowers and quickly moves closer to chat to Amy.

'What's wrong, Arlo? Jealous?' I ask, fluttering my eyelashes playfully at him.

'As a matter of fact,' he begins, turning back to me, 'outrageously so.'

My breath catching in my throat at the sincerity of his tone, I try to think of something to say, but apparently I've forgotten every word in the English language. He gestures for me to sit back down with him and I spend the whole time unable to concentrate on anything anyone is trying to say over the music. I'm too distracted by the way he's positioned himself: one arm holding me nestled against him; the other hand resting on the top of my thigh. At one point, Amy gestures that she wants a word, and I lean towards her to hear while Arlo chats to Jacob behind me, who appears to now be forgiven. Arlo's hand doesn't budge from around my waist as I bend forward.

'He's letting everyone know the score, isn't he,' Amy says with a giggle, slurring her words.

'What do you mean?'

'Arlo! He's telling the world you're together.'

'Amy, nothing's even happened yet.'

'Oh it will, my friend, it will,' she says firmly, patting my knee. 'I'm excited to hear all the details on the way back home tomorrow!'

Leaning back and laughing, I shake my head, but my heart flutters as Arlo feels me shuffling backwards and speeds up the process by pulling me back to him. I find his hand and link my fingers with his against my stomach. Amy's words have echoed my hopes, and when Jade and Michael come stumbling over to us to tell us they're heading home, those hopes skyrocket.

'Arlo, would you mind seeing my roommate home safely?' Jade cries, cupping his face with her hands. 'I am going to be seeing *your* roommate home safely, so tit for tat and all that.'

'Really?' Arlo says, raising his eyebrows, his warm, strong arm tightening round me. 'Well, if you insist—'

'Have fun, you two!' she trills, before turning to Michael. 'Let's go.'

'Okay,' Michael replies dreamily, following her out in wonder.

Neither of us makes a comment about it, sitting next to each other impatiently as the music thumps on, our hands intertwined. Finally, he asks if I want to leave and I nod, a lump rising in my throat. We don't bother to say goodbye to anyone as we exit. He orders an Uber on our way out and it arrives almost instantly. We sit by side in the car, not saying a word for the short journey to the hotel, the searing, restless tension between us filling the silence.

When we arrive, he jumps out and holds the door

open for me. I climb out and, taking his hand as he thanks the driver before shutting the door, I lead the way into the building and towards the lift. I press the button as he stands behind me, sliding one hand round my waist, and using his other to sweep my hair back across one shoulder so my neck is on show. I can feel his chest pressed against my back, rising heavily with each breath, steady and slow.

The lift pings open and I step in. He follows me closely. The doors shut behind us and he spins me round to face him. Wrapping my arms round his neck, I bite my lip and he buries his face in my hair with a satisfied sigh, pressing his lips against my shoulder.

He waits until I've let him into my room to make the move to finally kiss me after all tonight's teasing. One hand moving to the small of my back, the other gently tilts my jaw up until our lips touch. This kiss is different to before. When we kissed on that tequila-fuelled night, it was hard, fast and urgent. This kiss is achingly slow and soft, the kind that covers my skin in goosebumps and makes my whole body tremble with the anticipation of what's to come.

As my palms press against his solid chest, I start to become wildly impatient and deepen the kiss, arching into him. He responds instantly, letting out an involuntary groan as he kisses me harder, his hands sliding down my waist to grasp at my hips. My pulse quickening, I blindly search for the top button of his shirt, my fingers fumbling to open it and move down to the next. Breathing heavily, he breaks our kiss to look at me properly, his dark eyes reflecting my own longing.

'Are you sure?' he checks, his voice rugged and raspy.

'Yes,' I whisper, cradling his face in my hands and locking my eyes with his so he can be left in no doubt. 'I'm sure.'

Breaking into a smile, he reaches down to grab my thighs and lift me up, making me giggle as my legs automatically lock around his hips. He moves us towards the bed, easing me down gently. As he lowers himself on top of me and kisses me again, I close my eyes and hold him tightly, losing myself in the hope that I'll never have to let him go.

CHAPTER TWENTY

It's the middle of the night and Arlo's whispering something to me, but I'm so tired I don't really listen, smiling as he kisses me and then falling back asleep. When I wake up in the morning, I find him gone and Jade now in her bed across the room, still in her dress and make-up from last night, lying on her front above the duvet, snoring loudly. I check my phone, but there's no messages. Maybe he went for coffee? No, wait, it was dark out when he was talking to me; he must have gone back to his room. My heart sinks as I question why he didn't stay. I tell myself not to be so dramatic – we're in the same hotel as all our teammates and the coaches. It's understandable he didn't want everyone seeing him in the morning creeping back to his room. I'm guessing that's why Jade is back here, too.

Reaching out to grab a T-shirt and pyjama bottoms from my bag, I pull them on under the duvet and then tip-toe into our bathroom to shower and get dressed. I can't stop smiling thinking about last night. Under the hot water of the shower, my mind drifts to the way Arlo held me in the lift, the way he kissed me when we got back to the room, and how intoxicatingly sexy he is. Everything about last night was perfect, if only he'd been able to stay the whole night too. Once we're back in Durham and no longer in shared accommodation, that will be able to change. I shudder with excitement at the idea of a repeat of last night, biting my bottom lip. Now that I know my feelings are reciprocated, I just want to be with him *all the time*.

Once I'm ready for the day, I perch on the edge of Jade's bed and gently shake her awake. She emits a muffled groan into her pillow and reaches up to wipe her hair away from her face so she can squint at me.

'What time is it?' she croaks.

'Nine thirty. The coach leaves from outside at ten.' I

hold out a bottle of water. 'Here. Have some sips. While you shower, I'll go get us some coffee and meet you by the coach.'

'You are an angel sent from the Highlands to protect me.'

I grin as she hauls herself up and takes the bottled water. 'Fun night?' I ask.

'One of the better ones, although I'm paying for it now,' she admits, taking a swig. 'I never realised how hot Michael was before. I always thought he was very quiet and introverted. But, boy, does he know what he's doing.'

I giggle. 'It's always the quiet ones.'

'How was your night with Arlo? We passed in the corridor when we switched rooms and gave each other a high-five.'

'*Seriously?*'

'No,' she chortles. 'When he came back to his room at whatever time it was, I realised, despite my drunken state, that I didn't fancy waking up with two strikers in the room and felt it appropriate to return here. I'm glad he woke us up when he knocked on the door.'

'Thank goodness he knocked. He risked walking in on something.'

'You're telling me,' she says, raising her eyebrows.

She watches me curiously as I look down at my shoes with a frown.

'What's wrong? Don't tell me Arlo was shit in bed, because that would be such a—'

'No, no, he was … great,' I assure her. 'It was … amazing. I don't know why he left, that's all. I wondered whether you might have come back here and he felt he needed to go, but if you say that it was him who went back to his room first …'

She shrugs it off. 'I wouldn't worry, Sadie. He probably didn't want to field all the prying questions you'd get being seen leaving someone else's room. I can understand that.'

'Maybe.'

She reaches out to pat my hand with hers. 'You're reading into things, babe. He likes you. Anyone could see that last night. He couldn't take his eyes off you. It was like he was mesmerised. And who wouldn't be? The guy's got a brain.'

I break into a smile.

'Whenever he spotted you talking to some other guy, I thought his head might explode,' she continues, arching her brow. 'He's got it bad. So there's no chance he left this morning because he didn't want to spend the night with you. It will be because he feels a bit awkward us all being in the hotel or whatever. Trust me, when we're back in college, things will be different. We'll probably never get rid of him.'

'I hope so.' I sigh wistfully.

'Didn't I tell you that there was chemistry between you two right from the start?' she points out. 'I was right about that and I'm right about this. Trust me.'

'All right, sorry for being so pathetic.'

'You're not pathetic, my darling – you're just in love. Now,' she says, swinging her legs out of the bed, 'excuse me a second while I go throw up and question my life choices.'

As she stumbles into the bathroom, I sit frozen to the spot. I'm not sure which is more worrying: the fact that I'm clearly so into Arlo Hudson that Jade believes

I've fallen in love with him, or the idea that she might be right.

I try not to be annoyed or disappointed when Arlo doesn't sit next to me on the coach, but end up grappling with both emotions for the whole journey home. I tell myself that it's not a big deal and we're grown-ups, not teenagers in school – where you sit on the bus doesn't mean anything. What's more, everyone is so hungover and exhausted that no one cares where anyone else is sitting; they just want to put their headphones on and sleep. Even Hayley chooses to sit next to Quinn, putting her pink eye mask on and falling asleep against her friend's shoulder. I notice Dylan give her a strange look and then consequently plonk himself at the front of the coach, leaving the space next to him open for Arlo to take. Jade is one of the last to clamber up the steps and, as I hold her coffee aloft, she practically throws herself down the aisle towards it.

Things improve when I step off the coach to see Arlo waiting for me, having already fetched my bag from the hold.

'Hey,' he says, fidgeting with the bottom of his jacket. 'How was your journey?'

'I managed a bit of sleep. How about you?'

'Dylan likes to snuggle.'

I laugh. 'Lucky you. Maybe choose your travel partner a bit more wisely next time.'

'I'll be sure to. What are your plans today?' he asks hopefully.

'Jade wants to do a duvet day and watch all three *High School Musical* films,' I inform him, glancing back at where she's sat on top of her wheelie with her sunglasses on, scrolling through her phone mindlessly, waiting for me to finish. 'What's your plan?'

'A duvet day with movies sounds about right.' He hesitates, frowning, as though something is troubling him.

'Hey, is everything okay?' I ask, panicking that he's regretting what happened.

'Yeah,' he says breezily. 'It's ... uh ... last night ...'

He trails off, shifting his weight. Heat rises up my neck to my face as I watch him search for the words to say whatever he wants to say and, judging from his troubled expression, I brace myself for him to tell me it was a huge mistake.

'It was really fun,' he lands on eventually.

I nod. 'I thought so.'

'Yeah?' he checks, his shoulders easing at my comment. 'Good.'

It dawns on me that he's somehow worried I didn't enjoy last night, or maybe I'm the one regretting it this morning.

'*Really* fun,' I say, just to drive home the point.

It works. His whole body relaxes and he looks up at me, breaking into a wide grin.

'So, exactly how long are these *High School Musical* films?' he asks, arching his brow. 'Do you think you'll still be watching them tonight? Or do you think you might have time to … watch something else with someone else?'

A warmth fills my stomach. After a long journey questioning whether last night was a one-time thing, I feel the weight of worry lift as relief begins to sink in. He left early and didn't sit next to me on the coach, but he's waited for me afterwards to ask me to hang out with him. That can't mean I'm alone in this.

'Arlo,' I begin coyly, 'are you asking me to watch a movie with you tonight?'

'If you're around, then, yeah, why not?' he says with a shrug.

'You're not going to make us watch an old black-and-white film, are you?'

'You can choose the movie,' he promises.

'Nah, you choose,' I insist. 'You're the film buff. Didn't you once tell me that you could give me a list of films I *had* to watch? So, go ahead and pick something that will change my life.'

'Jeez, no pressure, then,' he says, putting his hands in his pockets.

'What's the matter, Hudson?' I grin, picking up my bag and walking away to call back to him over my shoulder. 'I thought you liked challenges.'

CHAPTER TWENTY-ONE

I've always been impatient. I know it's one of my flaws. When I'm waiting on something, it's all I can think about and I can't bring myself to focus on anything else no matter how hard I try. Since I set my heart on a football career, nothing else has really mattered. Nothing else has seemed anywhere near as important.

Until him.

When I'm not with Arlo, I can't stop thinking about him, wondering what he's up to and when I'll get to see him next. I can't figure out which I enjoyed more: the night in Nottingham or the night after, when he showed up at my door with popcorn and we snuggled into the duvet together and watched a film about an heiress and a leopard called *Bringing Up Baby* starring Katharine Hepburn. I wasn't convinced I was going to like such an old movie, but it was hilarious. I loved it, and when I told Arlo that as the credits rolled, he looked so pleased with himself. It was adorable.

'I *knew* you'd like it,' he'd said smugly. 'I just knew.'

'Because you guessed I liked comedies?'

He'd shifted himself down and I'd rolled in to face him.

'Because you have excellent taste,' he'd said, before kissing me.

Waking up the next morning wrapped in his arms, our bodies entangled beneath the sheets, I'd felt deliriously happy. As he slept soundly, I'd studied his long, dark eyelashes, the gentle slope of his nose, his full lips, and I'd allowed myself to hope that there would be many more mornings of waking up to him. Resting my head on his chest, listening to his heartbeat, I felt safe for the first time in a long time. The truth is, ever since my dad got his diagnosis, I've felt alone in my worries, marching through life with one goal and a hell of a lot of expectation. But when

I'm with Arlo, it's like I can just *be*. I can breathe again.

My impatience is getting the better of me, though. It's naive to think we can jump into whatever this is head first, simply because I'm sure. While I can acknowledge that he's letting his guard down with me too, I'm learning quickly that he's more cautious, taking things at a slower pace than I'd like. He doesn't message often and, since the movie night, he hasn't stayed over or suggested a date night. I'd tried to imply that we should hang out again, but he'd had a busy week and I couldn't fault him for being sociable.

Reminding me that boys are useless with their phones, Jade keeps telling me to relax and enjoy it, but there's nothing enjoyable about checking your phone for a message that isn't coming or waiting for someone you like to ask you on a date. When we have our private practice session, he's his usual fun and flirtatious self, but we keep the focus mainly on the football. That should make me happy; that's how it *should* be. Football has always come first for me. But it's not how I want it to be at all. I want him to ask me to cancel practice so we can go out instead. I want him to kiss me on the pitch without a care who sees.

I want *him*. And I want him to want me.

But we don't always get what we want, as I find out one afternoon later that week just before our team practice. The atmosphere in the changing room is fun and upbeat after another win for us two days earlier – and not just us, but the boys, too. Arlo gave an assist to Michael in the first half and scored two goals in the second half of their match. Their team has distinctly improved and their position in the league looks safe.

'Did you see Michael on Wednesday?' Quinn teases Jade, grinning at her as she shoves her bag in her locker. 'I've never seen him play like that before. Anyone would think he's trying to impress someone.'

'Don't give me that look, Quinn. We are *not* a thing,' Jade insists, rolling her eyes.

'He's cute,' Amy comments, leaning against the wall as she waits for us to finish getting ready. 'Has he been messaging you?'

She shrugs. 'A little.'

'If you and Michael start dating, we'll have an adorable pattern emerging of pairing off the football boys with the football girls,' Quinn remarks, prompting Jade to snort. 'I'm going to find it hard to keep up with all these relationships. Hayley and Dylan, Sadie and Arlo, Jade and Michael . . . who's next?'

'Excuse you, we are *not* in a relationship,' Jade clarifies, chucking a sock at Quinn, who dodges it while chuckling at her own comment.

'Neither are we,' I mutter, trying not to sound too bitter about it.

'Arlo hasn't asked you to be exclusive?' Amy says, looking surprised.

I shake my head.

'Of course he hasn't,' Hayley chimes up from where she's checking her reflection in the mirror. 'They're not *serious.*'

I start, pausing midway through tying my bootlaces. Quinn and Amy share a look. Maya looks stunned, and Jade is downright furious.

'*Hayley,*' Jade snaps, putting her hands on her hips, 'why would you say that?'

Flushing, Hayley spins round and stares at me wide-eyed.

'Oh my god, I wasn't saying that as though it was my personal opinion – I'm so sorry if you thought that,' she explains innocently. 'I was repeating what Arlo said!'

A lump forms in my throat.

'Arlo said that?' I croak, trying and failing to sound casual about it.

She nods. 'Yeah, last night when we were out at Osbournes. There was a bunch of us there. Dylan invited me, so I went with Quinn, and there were a few of the football boys and some girls from Arlo's college, I think.'

When I messaged Arlo yesterday to ask what he was up to, he'd said he was having a boys night. He didn't invite me to join.

'There's this friend of Arlo's who is clearly into him – I think she plays for the thirds, actually,' Hayley continues, 'so Dylan was asking him if there was anything going on with her, and obviously I stepped in and reminded him about you, Sadie, because I've got your back. When Dylan teased him about you being his girlfriend, Arlo said that you two weren't serious.' She pauses, blinking at me. 'I assumed that you both felt that way. Otherwise he wouldn't have said that in front of me, right? He would know that, being your friend, I'd tell you he was going around telling people that you two weren't anything serious.'

I nod slowly. 'Right. Yeah. Makes sense.'

The changing room falls into uncomfortable silence. Quinn is looking at the floor, and Amy and Maya are watching me with concerned expressions. I feel strangely numb. My brain seems to be taking its time to process her words. As it dawns on me how stupid I've been and how far I've let myself fall, I grow hot with the mortification, and tears begin to prick at my eyes. For it to be Hayley who has delivered this news is the cherry on the cake. Here I am in front of her, the fool once again.

What an idiot.

'Sadie—' Jade begins.

'What? I'm good!' I insist, finishing my lace and standing up to shut my locker. 'We're not serious – he's right. This isn't a big deal. Let's get out there and play before Coach Hendricks loses his head.'

Before anyone can respond, I rush out of the changing room, grateful for the cold air hitting my face as I burst out of the door and run into the field.

The boys aren't training with us today, thank god, and I try not to get distracted by the sight of Arlo throwing himself into the drills a couple of pitches over. At one point, he's standing on the sideline and he catches my eye as I position myself to practise a cross. He waves. Turning away from him and scowling, I run up to the ball and kick it way too hard.

'Get it together, McGrath!' Coach Hendricks calls out to me, ducking as it soars over his head on the other side of the pitch.

He couldn't be more right. I've let myself forget what's important and what I'm doing here. I knew Arlo Hudson was bad news from the start – and what's happened? I've let myself fall for his charm, like every other sucker, and it's left my stomach twisting in anguish waiting on his replies and distracted from my game as I daydream about him.

Well, not any more. Lesson learnt. I won't be played by him again.

When training finishes, Coach Hendricks asks me to stay behind while everyone else heads back in. Jade looks torn, lingering by the sideline, but I tell her I'll see her afterwards, shooting her a confident smile to communicate that I'm okay.

'What are you, her babysitter, Grosvenor?' Coach Hendricks barks.

She reluctantly leaves, promising me she'll wait for me so we can walk back to Collingwood together.

'Are you all right?' Coach asks, watching her go and then turning to me with his brow furrowed. 'You seemed ... upset today.'

'No, I'm fine,' I tell him. 'In fact, I've never felt more determined. Any feedback from my performance today?'

'Keeping the ball in play on this pitch rather than trying to kick it all the way to Australia would be my first note,' he says wryly.

I grimace. 'Got it. Sorry about that.'

'Look, you know how important the next couple of weeks are for this team. You win this season, you make history, and that's no mean feat. We're top of the league, but only by one point. We can't get complacent.'

'I know that, Coach.'

He rubs his chin, looking out over the field. 'There's going to be a scout watching these last two matches. I've mentioned you to him and he's interested. He's got a lot of connections, McGrath. You need to show him what you can do.'

I nod, my mouth dry and my breath shaky.

'Don't worry, we'll make sure he sees the best of you,' Coach assures me firmly. 'You're playing well at the moment, but I want to see you go with your gut a bit more. Trust in yourself as much as you trust strategy and tactics. Don't rely so much on this –' he taps the side of his head and then moves his hand down to his chest, over his heart – 'and play with a bit more of this.'

'Got it,' I tell him. 'I won't let you down.'

'Nothing to do with me, McGrath,' he says, frowning. 'Don't play for other people. Play for yourself.'

I look down at my boots.

'Coach, since these next two games are so important to the team and to my career, I think it would be best if I put all my effort and time into my own personal training. As much as I'd like to help Arlo Hudson, I think it's best if we end our practices together.'

He arches his brow. 'Oh? I thought you two were . . . close.'

My cheeks flush with heat. Bloody hell, even the *coaches* knew. How obvious was I?!

'We've seen improvement from both of you since you started your private training,' he continues brazenly, 'and as you know, I strongly believe that it's better to train with a partner than solo. But he has come along nicely, and if you think it would be better to conclude the training here—'

'I do,' I state. 'I don't think there's anything we can do for each other any more. He's playing well and I'm better off alone.'

Looking a little taken aback at my stern tone, he proceeds to nod.

'All right, McGrath. You're off the hook.' He hesitates, adding, 'Thank you for taking the time to practise with him. I know Coach Nevile has greatly appreciated it, and I'm sure Hudson is grateful to you, too.'

'Thanks, Coach,' I say, before heading off to the changing rooms.

When Arlo messages the next day, my heart skips at the sight of his name appearing on my screen and I shake my head, disappointed in myself. I take a deep breath and begin to type my reply.

Arlo
Hey, after our practice today
do you want to grab a drink?
Think some of the others will be out too
We can meet them after xx

Sadie
I've been meaning to message
you actually
Coach said there was no
need to continue our training

sessions for the rest of the
season.
You can talk to him if you have
any questions.
And thanks, but I'm busy
tonight

I press send. The blue ticks appear immediately, so I
know he's read it.

My phone starts ringing. It's him.

I ignore his call.

CHAPTER TWENTY-TWO

'It's Sadie, right?'

I glance up from my laptop to see a girl leaning her hand on the free chair opposite mine, looking at me hopefully with her big hazel eyes. Petite and girl-next-door pretty, with freckles smattered across her nose and long, wavy brown hair, she looks familiar, but I can't place her.

'I'm Ellie,' she tells me hurriedly. 'I think we've met on a night out before. You're friends with Hayley, right? I play football too. I'm on the thirds.'

'Oh, hey,' I say, smiling warmly up at her. 'How are you?'

'Good. You?'

'Fine, thanks.'

We fall into silence as I watch her expectantly. She bites her lip, tapping her nails against the chair impatiently.

'Did you want the seat? You can take it if you like,' I offer, although it does seem a bit strange, considering there are other free tables across the cafe. 'I'm not waiting for anyone and I'm going to be leaving in a bit anyway to get to a lecture.'

'Oh! No, I ... uh ... I don't need the chair. Actually, I wanted to ask you something.'

'Okay,' I say, leaning back. 'What do you need? Is it a football question?'

She dips her head, blushing. 'Not exactly. It's ... about Arlo Hudson.'

My smile freezes. 'What about him?'

'Oh god, this is awkward. I'm sorry, I'm being so embarrassing,' she says, running a hand through her hair. 'Basically, I was wondering if you two were, like, a thing. Because I was thinking of asking him out, but if he's already taken, then obviously I wouldn't go there because ... girl code.' She grimaces. 'Argh!

Cringe. Sorry. You're probably together and I've just completely embarrassed myself.'

I exhale, my heart hammering against my chest.

'Don't be sorry,' I say, glancing down at my hands in my lap. 'You haven't embarrassed yourself. Actually, it's pretty decent of you to ask.'

She smiles gratefully at me, her cheeks glowing pink.

'We're not together,' I confirm for her. 'So you can go ahead and ask him out.'

She gasps excitedly. 'Great! Okay, cool. Sorry, I wasn't sure if you guys were still . . . Anyway, I'm glad I asked. Thank you so much.'

'No problem. Good luck.'

'Thanks,' she says cheerily, straightening. 'And good luck for your last two matches. You're top of the league, right? No surprises there. I'm sure it will stay that way. See you around!'

'See you,' I say, as she spins around and dances out the door.

Closing my laptop, I glumly gather my things together and head out the cafe to slowly meander to my lecture. I'll be early, but there's no chance I can concentrate on work now, so no point in hanging around here. I'm a few metres from the door when someone purposefully stands in my way, forcing me to look up from the ground.

Shit.

'Hey, Sadie,' Arlo says, his brow furrowed. 'Jade said you might be here.'

I pull the strap of my bag up my shoulder as it comes loose, and step around him.

'Sorry, I have to go – I'm late for my lecture,' I mutter.

'You've been avoiding me,' he accuses, falling into step with me. 'What's going on?'

'Nothing. I haven't been avoiding you.'

'I've tried calling, and you haven't replied to any of my messages.'

'I've been busy.'

He reaches out to grab my arm and bring me to a stop.

'Sadie, come on,' he pleads, as I glance around us, desperate to avoid eye contact. 'Talk to me. Please?'

With a heavy sigh, I force myself to look at him. He smiles at me.

'Hey,' he says gently, acknowledging my meeting his eyes for the first time this conversation. I steel myself, refusing to wilt under his affectionate gaze.

It's a game. He's playing you.

'Arlo, I have nothing to say,' I tell him coldly. 'The season is almost over and Coach agreed that I should focus on my own practice from now on. You don't need me.'

He frowns. 'Okay, if that's the general consensus. I disagree, but if you would rather we call it quits—'

'I would.'

He hesitates, narrowing his eyes at me. 'What's going on? Everything was . . . great between us and now we're . . . Look, have I done something to upset you?'

'Why would anything you do upset me?' I ask, tilting my head. 'It's not like we're together. We're nothing serious, right?'

He blinks at me. 'I . . . well, no, but—'

'I'm glad we're on the same page. Oh, I met your friend Ellie just now in the cafe. We had a nice chat and I hope things work out between you two. Not that it's any of my business, but don't mess her around, okay?

She seems really sweet and wouldn't deserve that. Anyway –' I check the time on my phone – 'I have to run. See you around.'

Leaving him standing there speechless, I turn on my heel and walk away, fighting the urge to look back. I've already made up my mind that I can't be friends with Arlo. I've tried it before and it didn't work. With us, it has to be all or nothing. Now at least both of us know the score. We're nothing.

Why is he here?

It's not fair. Arlo is not supposed to be here in the stand, cheering us on in our penultimate fixture. Shouldn't he be out with his friends or his new girlfriend? Or focusing on his own football? He has no right to be here, watching our match. He must have shown up midway through the first half. I spotted him at half-time. He gave me a weak smile, but I scowled at him as we moved in for a huddle.

It's still nil–nil and I have to focus. I can't let him distract me. There's a scout somewhere among the spectators who could change everything for me. And this isn't just a big game for me personally, but also for the whole team. If we beat Loughborough today, we could win the league, so long as Edinburgh lose the game they're currently playing.

I clap as Hayley does an excellent slide tackle, sending the ball off the attacking player's heel and out of play. She takes the throw-in, looking for a player in space. My eyes flicker across to the sideline where he's standing with his hands in his jacket pockets. He's staring right at me. I quickly look away.

Why does he have to look so good?

Hayley's thrown it to Alisha, who's working hard to find Amy, but her opponent is aggressively pressurising her and goes for the tackle, sending it away. I groan in disappointment. Out of the corner of my eye, I see Arlo greet a couple of people who have just arrived in the stand to watch the game. I can't help but curiously glance over, my chest tightening when I see it's Ellie and her friend. She's smiling at something Arlo is saying, reaching out to touch his arm lightly.

What is wrong with them? Do they have to come here and rub it in my face?

A cheer goes up from the home crowd and I tear my eyes away from Arlo to see that Amy has the ball. And I haven't moved. Flustered, I race in as Amy spots me and whips the ball into the box. By some miracle, the Loughborough team defender is out of position and I have a free header.

I send the ball miles over the bar.

Amy had already started celebrating, but her face crumples and she buries her head in her arms. I stare at the goal in disbelief, breathing heavily, my hands on my hips. The Loughborough keeper is clapping her hands in relief, but shouting instructions at her defenders to not let that happen again. Someone gives me a comforting pat on the back.

'Next time,' Hayley's voice says in my ear. 'You'll get it next time.'

But everyone knows you don't get many chances like that. There might not be a next time this match. That was my chance to get ahead.

And I missed.

The game resumes, but my hands are trembling still from the shock and embarrassment. Coach Hendricks is yelling at me to keep focused, but the deep lines etched into his forehead tell me that he's as confused as I am. Soon the shock is replaced by anger at Arlo for coming here and ruining everything. This is his fault.

I hate him.

He may have hurt me badly, but I won't let him ruin my career. I try to channel all my frustration into motivation to get another chance at goal and prove to the scout that I made a rare mistake. Loughborough seems to have a fresh wave of confidence from my miss, their team playing more aggressively as they move the ball into a dangerous area. Amy and I fall back to help, and I race towards the midfielder dribbling the ball, going for the tackle.

As her legs go out from under her and she falls to the ground, the whistle blows.

'I barely touched her!' I argue, but it's no use.

It's ruled a careless, mistimed tackle, and I've given away a free kick.

Their midfield and centre forward step up to take it. The centre forward rolls the ball a few metres to the left, passing it to the outside of our team's wall, while the midfielder runs and strikes it.

I watch helplessly as the ball flies past the wall and into the top right-hand corner of the goal.

CHAPTER TWENTY-THREE

Mum places a coffee down in front of me and takes the seat next to me at the kitchen table, clasping her steaming mug of tea.

'You're awfully quiet,' she remarks, watching me curiously.

I take a sip of my drink. 'Pre-match nerves, that's all.'

'Nerves are good,' she tells me, reaching out to pat my hand, before turning to Dad. 'Isn't that right? You always got nervous before a game and I'd say the same. You want the adrenaline keeping you alert and on your toes.'

Dad nods. 'That's right. What's the match tomorrow?'

'Sadie has her final,' Mum explains patiently, even

though I know she would have told him this already. 'It's an away match against Edinburgh. That's why she's here. She's come up a day early to spend some time with us, which is wonderful.'

'Ach, you'll easy beat Hibs,' Dad says, tapping his finger on the table decisively. 'You need to capitalise on their defensive lapses. They keep making the same mistakes recently.'

'No, Dad, we're not playing against Hibernian,' I tell him quietly. 'This is the university league. We're playing against Edinburgh Uni.'

'It's a very important match,' Mum informs him.

'Oh?' he says, looking at me for an explanation.

'They're ahead of us in the league now on goal difference,' I explain, my eyes falling to the table. 'We lost to Loughborough and they drew their last game. So, we need to win the final by two goals to win the league.'

'You can do it,' Mum insists, giving me an encouraging smile. 'We'll be there cheering you on. We have every faith in you.'

I shake my head. 'I messed up. Edinburgh is a great

team and I threw away our chance at going into this game with the advantage. I ruined everything and now we'll probably lose.'

Mum leans across the table to take my hand in hers. 'Don't say that, Sadie.'

There's no point in Mum trying to make me feel better. At this point, I'm not sure anything will. When the referee blew the whistle at the end of the Loughborough game, I couldn't move. Bending over double to rest my hands on my knees, bowing my head, my ears were ringing with the pain and disappointment of my mistakes, drowning out their cheers of celebration. Jade came over to rest her hand on my back, telling me that it was okay, but I didn't believe her. My whole body ached and my eyes filled with tears. When I finally managed to force myself to move, I shook hands with the opposing team in a zombie-like state. I walked off the pitch without a glance at Arlo. In the changing rooms, I sat on the bench and didn't budge.

The rest of my team were so nice about it. They told me that it wasn't my fault, that the team just hadn't pulled together like we'd needed to. They gave me supportive, encouraging comments. We could still win the league, it wasn't over, they said. But their words bounced off me, ineffective and hopeless. I eventually got showered and dressed, not saying a word to anyone. Jade had obviously told them about the scout, so they all shot me pitying looks as I got ready.

'Arlo is outside,' Jade had told me cautiously, coming back in as I'd picked up my bag to leave. 'He said he'd like to talk to you.'

'Please tell him to go,' I'd whispered, closing my eyes and leaning against the wall. 'I don't want to talk to anyone, Jade, least of all him.'

She'd nodded and walked out ahead of me. A few minutes later, she'd returned to tell me he was gone and the coast was clear. That evening, he'd sent me a message to say sorry and that he hoped I was okay. He was here if I needed him, he said.

He was the last person I needed.

I wanted to blame it all on him, and at first I did, but when I woke up the next morning, I knew the blame lay at my door. I'd let myself lose focus and become caught up in him being there. I'd let the nerves of the scout's presence get the better of me. The only person at fault was me. I'd let my team down. I'd let Coach Hendricks down. I'd let myself down.

The weight of it all has been unbearable.

It's been a tough few days.

'You shouldn't come to the game tomorrow,' I tell my parents miserably. 'I don't want to let you down, too.'

'Sadie,' Mum says, looking pained, 'you could never let us down! We're so proud of you and everything you do.'

'Yes, we are very proud, Sadie,' Dad says with a nod, and the fact that he communicates it so clearly and sincerely brings me to tears.

'You wouldn't have been if you'd seen me play in my last match, Dad,' I admit, a tear rolling down my cheek. Mum squeezes my hand. 'I made so many mistakes. I let the pressure get to me and my head was in a spin. If we don't win the league, it will be my fault.'

To my surprise, Dad lets out an amused grunt.

'Celtic,' he says, causing me and Mum to share a look.

'What's that, Dad?' I ask gently, my heart sinking as I steel myself for him to spiral into a state of confusion.

'I was at Celtic,' he says impatiently.

'Yes, for a time,' Mum says, wondering where he's going with this.

'We were playing Dumbarton and I had a bad game, missed a penalty.' He shakes his head, frowning at the memory. 'It was terrible, terrible. Wanted to throw in the towel. Later in the season, I scored a hat trick against Dundee and a brace against Motherwell.' His expression eases and he looks up at me, his eyes glistening. 'Each game is a new game.'

Wiping away my tears, I break into a watery smile.

'Thanks, Dad,' I whisper. 'I needed to hear that.'

The doorbell rings and Mum lets go of my hand to go and answer it. Still smiling appreciatively at Dad, I take another sip of my coffee. We hear Mum talking to whoever it is before she encourages them to come in, stepping back into the kitchen a few moments later.

'It's your friend from uni, Sadie,' she says brightly.

I almost choke on my coffee as Arlo follows her into the room.

'Arlo!' I splutter, clattering my mug down on the table and getting to my feet. 'What are you doing here?'

'Sorry for intruding,' he begins cheerily, holding a bouquet of flowers. 'I came to the city a little earlier than the rest of the team, and Jade mentioned you were here – I thought I'd stop by. I hope that's okay.'

'Of course!' Mum says, her eyes drifting down him slowly and back up again. 'You are very welcome. Sadie has mentioned you, Arlo.'

'Has she?' he says, grinning at me while I glare at Mum. He hands her the flowers. 'These are for you, Mrs McGrath.'

'How beautiful!' she says, her cheeks flushing pink. Looks like I'm not the only McGrath to fall for the charm of Arlo Hudson. 'That's very thoughtful of you.'

He turns to Dad, holding out his hand. 'Nice to meet you, sir.'

'You're a friend of Sadie's?' Dad asks warily, shaking his hand.

'Arlo is at Durham, too, Dad. He's, uh, a-a striker on the men's team,' I stammer, still trying to get my head round the fact that he's here.

'A fellow footballer, good lad,' Dad says approvingly.

'It's an honour to meet you,' Arlo says. 'Your daughter has been kind enough to give up a lot of her time to train me up this season.'

'Has she?' Dad raises his eyebrows. 'Sadie is a big talent. Always has been.'

'Anyway,' I jump in, before things can get too gushy, 'why are you here? I mean, how come you decided to come to Edinburgh early?'

'I've never been and I wanted to see the sights,' he explains. 'You sold it to me as an impressive place, so I wanted to see it for myself. I didn't think we'd have much time to explore tomorrow.'

'Oh, it's a beautiful city, isn't it, Sadie?' Mum enthuses, busying herself by fetching a vase and filling it with water. 'And the best way to see it is with a local guide.'

'You know where I can find one of those?' Arlo asks hopefully.

Mum turns off the tap and nods to me. 'Right here.'

I blink at her. 'Huh?'

'You were just saying that you wanted to take a

walk around the city today, weren't you, Sadie? Get some fresh air and clear your head before the match tomorrow,' she says brazenly, looking for some scissors to start cutting the stems. 'Why don't you take Arlo around? Show him the best spots.'

'That would be great,' Arlo says, beaming at me.

'I . . . uh . . . okay,' I hear myself say.

'Off you go, then,' Mum bosses, ushering me up off my chair. 'So lovely to meet you, Arlo. Enjoy our city, and perhaps you'd like to join us for dinner tonight?'

'Arlo has the team dinner tonight, Mum,' I say hurriedly, grabbing my coat. 'He won't be able to—'

'I'd love to join you,' he answers.

'But . . . but won't you want to be with the team to discuss tactics and stuff for tomorrow?' I squeak, looking at him wide-eyed.

He nods to Dad. 'I imagine I'll learn a lot more about the beautiful game here than I would speaking with any of my team.'

Dad chuckles. 'Happy to give a few pointers.'

'See you tonight, then,' Mum confirms. 'Enjoy today. Bye, Sadie!'

'Bye,' I say, tripping over my feet as I lead the way out of the front door, still not sure what the hell is going on or how I've ended up in this situation.

'Looking forward to this evening, thank you,' Arlo calls out over his shoulder as Mum smiles to herself while she closes the door behind him. He turns to me as I stand on the pavement in a daze. 'Thanks for this, Sadie.'

'What are you doing here?' I blurt out, frowning.

'I told you, I wanted to see the—'

'I mean, why are you *here*?' I clarify, nodding to my house.

He pauses, before saying quietly, 'I wanted to see you.'

My eyes fall to the ground. I sniff, shoving my hands in my pockets.

'I'msosorryaboutyourmatchagainstLoughborough,' he continues. 'I was worried about you and you haven't been answering my calls. I wanted to make sure you're okay.' He hesitates. 'If you want me to leave, I will. But I know tomorrow is a huge deal for you, and I guess I didn't want you to be alone.'

I exhale, kicking nervously at the pavement with the toe of my shoe.

'Sadie, forget about everything else – everything that's ... happened between us,' he pleads. 'Let someone be there for you. Let *me* be there for you.' He sighs, running a hand through his hair. 'I just want to know if you're okay.'

Taking a deep breath, I force myself to look up at him.

'I'm terrified,' I whisper.

'I know,' he says, stepping closer to me. His hand twitches as though he's considering reaching out to me, but he thinks better of it. 'Let me know what you want me to do. Tell me how I can help. Anything you want, we'll do. We can talk about it, not talk about it, sit somewhere, walk around, see the sights ... We could go to the castle and try to find a hawk to chase you around to boost your fitness—'

I burst out laughing. He breaks into a satisfied smile.

'Whatever you want to do, we'll do it,' he concludes.

I sigh heavily. 'Okay. Let's go see some sights and not talk about football. Or anything important.'

'Okay.' He nods. 'We'll talk about unimportant things. Not a problem. I happen to be an expert at talking shit.'

'I noticed.'

'Now there's a glimpse of the Sadie I know: quick, dry and scathing.' He grins at me, rubbing his hands together. 'So, one day in Edinburgh. Where shall we go first?'

CHAPTER TWENTY-FOUR

Just breathe.

Mum's voice echoes around my head as I shake my hands out having won the coin toss. It's a cold, drizzly day and all the spectators are wrapped up in their coats, hoods up. It's a blessing. It means I can't see him among them, even though I know he's there. His match isn't until later today, and all the men's team are here to support us.

Stop thinking about Arlo.

I know exactly where Mum and Dad are, sitting in the front row of the stand, watching me intently. I was so consumed by my nerves earlier that I could hardly eat breakfast until Mum reminded me sternly that I needed the fuel to play my best. She took one glance at my shaking hand as I reached for my glass of water and smiled warmly at me.

'Nerves are good, remember? Like I would tell your dad before a big game,' she said, coming to stand over me and rubbing my back. 'Just breathe.'

Watching the Edinburgh team move into position, I inhale deeply. Dad wasn't on his best form this morning, becoming confused when Mum told him they were off to watch the football. But I try to focus on his words to me yesterday, rather than his puzzled expression as he saw me head out this morning with my sports bag.

Each game is a new game.

I exhale slowly. Just because I felt like a failure after the last match, it doesn't mean I'll be a failure in this one. I have to hold on to that. Somewhere in that stand is a scout who will make a decision today that could change my life. All I can hope is that if he was left unimpressed by my last performance, he gives me the chance to change his mind with this one.

The referee steps up to place the ball in the centre spot.

My throat tightens. I feel sick. Normally, I'm a bit nervous before play begins, but I'm never this nervous. There's too much pressure, too much riding on this game. I swallow, glancing up at the stand.

Where is he?

I have no right to depend on him for today. Nothing has changed. He's not my boyfriend. Yesterday, he was true to his word and we didn't talk about anything important, as I requested. As reluctant as I was at first to spend time with him after everything that's happened between us, I ended up having such a good time and feeling grateful for his intrusion. If he hadn't turned up, I would have spent the day probably spiralling into a state of worry about today.

Instead, I was able to forget about everything while I became an Edinburgh tour guide for the day, wandering around the cobbled streets of the Old Town, giggling at Arlo's dorky enthusiasm for the numerous literary landmarks. He took a ridiculous number of pictures of Ian Rankin's handprints in the flagstones by the City Chambers courtyard and then insisted that we go for a drink in the Conan Doyle, the pub near the house where Arthur Conan Doyle was born, making me take several pictures of him next to the Sherlock Holmes statue down the road. I burst out laughing when he struck up the same pose as the statue, pretending to hold a pipe.

Come to think of it, I spent a lot of the day laughing.

My parents adored him. Mum told me as much after dinner, when he'd left to go back to his hotel. I shouldn't have been surprised – it's hard for anyone to dislike Arlo. As ever, he was charming and interesting and helpful. But I could tell he was making an extra effort with my family yesterday. He'd clearly done his research and engaged Dad in a conversation about his career, being patient with him when he struggled with what he was trying to say, and showing sincere interest when he was talking. He made Dad laugh when he was self-deprecating about his own talents and when he talked about American soccer.

Needless to say, Mum fell head over heels for him.

'He is gorgeous, isn't he?' she'd hissed to me when he went to the bathroom.

'Mum! Shush! He might hear you!'

'I'm sure he's heard it before,' she'd said defensively, swirling her wine around her glass. 'Beckham would be jealous of that jaw. And those eyes!'

'Mum, *please.*'

'I'm just saying. But you know what I like about him the most?'

I'd groaned, burying my face in my hands. 'Please god, don't say something like ... his butt.'

'His butt is very nice, yes, but that's not what I was going to say,' she'd clarified. 'What I like most about him is how much he cares about my daughter. Anyone can see he's smitten.'

Last night, I lay in bed staring at the ceiling wondering why everything was so easy with Arlo, yet so complicated between us. That's when it hit me that I'd never actually asked him that outright and I probably should have done. He may have been unfair to brush off whatever was between us to Dylan and Hayley, but maybe it was also unfair of me not to have a frank conversation with him about it when I was so bothered by it. I never gave him the chance to explain how he felt. I never told him how I felt.

I shouldn't have spent yesterday talking about nothing. I should have got answers. Then at least I'd know. Rather than be standing here on the pitch at the beginning of the final, wondering why we can't seem to get it right, when I should be focusing on my game.

'Ready?' the referee says, glancing at me. I nod.

The whistle blows and the match begins.

I kick the ball back to Hayley, before pushing up the pitch looking for space. The defender is giving me no breathing room, marking me brilliantly. I wince when Hayley makes a sloppy pass and loses the ball, but, considering my own mistakes recently, I can't be annoyed. I know she can win it back.

Hayley and Dylan have broken up. Jade mentioned it to me this morning and was surprised at my disappointed reaction.

'Sadie, you should be secretly pleased about this,' she'd muttered. 'I know you think she's the best thing ever, but no ex is not just a *little* bit happy to hear that the rebound didn't work out. Admit it. She flaunted him in front of you.'

'Honestly, I really don't care about that any more,'

I'd informed her. 'I feel sad for her and, selfishly, I don't want her to be distracted today. Dealing with heartbreak isn't what you want going into a final.'

Jade had snorted. 'Heartbreak? Hayley broke up with *him* after getting with someone else. Twice. She told him she hoped they could be friends.'

As captain, I'd still felt it appropriate to check that she was okay before we went out on the pitch, making sure she felt supported. She'd smiled when I explained why I was asking and reached up to cradle my face in her hands.

'Sadie, you are an amazing person.' She'd dropped her hands and sighed, looking down at the floor. 'I'm sorry if I ever hurt you. Really.'

I'd shrugged. 'Hey, it's all good. We're friends. I'm not just saying that.'

'Likewise, and if Arlo is stupid enough to let you go, then that will be his biggest regret,' she'd said with a smile, bringing her eyes up to meet mine. 'And I'm not just saying that.'

I bring my focus back to the game when the ball comes into Alisha's possession.

She carves through the centre of Edinburgh's defence and suddenly the ball is at my feet. I run towards the keeper, our first opportunity of the match. The keeper rushes me and I try to chip the ball over her, but she gets a hand to it. The ball goes out for a corner. Trying not to feel too deflated, I jostle for position as Hayley takes the corner, but a defender heads it back up the pitch.

Later in the game, I find myself on my own on the wing. Quinn chips the ball over the defender into the right corner and I run over to it, my heart racing. I have space, so cut in towards the goal. I have the opportunity to shoot on my left foot – I hesitate. I see Amy making a run to the back post and make the decision to play it safe and pass it. The ball is easily picked up by a central defender. As it's sent back down the other end, we race after it, but the Edinburgh team are too good and one of their strikers is in a great space. Their right-winger crosses it to her and she shoots. The ball soars just over Maya's fingertips, hitting the back of the net.

One–nil.

The whistle blows for half-time. My heart sinks.

CHAPTER TWENTY-FIVE

A quick scan around the room at my teammates' faces confirms that my feeling of dejection and despair is shared. Coach Hendricks is giving us a pep talk, telling us that the game isn't over yet and there's still time to win it back. No one looks convinced by his encouragement. It's hard to believe, when we're one–nil down at half-time, we'll be able to beat this team by two goals. Having run through some strategy points, Coach claps his hands together so loudly it makes us jump. I snap my head up to look at him.

'Forget about the league,' he tells us, brushing it off with a wave of his hand. 'This is your final game of the season. This is the last time that you're going to play together. There have been some fantastic moments of play today and throughout the season. You should be immensely proud of yourselves. You're a great team and it's a privilege to be your coach. For the rest of this game, enjoy working together and playing to each other's strengths. Help each other to show off. This is your last chance to do so, after all.'

'Nah, I'm sure we'll find other opportunities to show off, Coach,' Jade says, prompting a laugh from the team.

'I don't doubt it with you, Grosvenor.' He sighs, rolling his eyes. 'Look, I believe that this team can win this match. But that's not enough. You lot have to believe that, too. Whether or not you win today, you've been on a journey as a team . . .' He hesitates, frowning. 'I'm thinking of a song. What is it?' He clicks his fingers. '"The Climb". That's the one.'

Maya squints at him. 'The Miley Cyrus song?'

He nods. 'Yep.'

'You . . . listen to Miley Cyrus?' Hayley checks, trying to fight a smile.

He shrugs, unfazed. 'It's a great song with a message

that we can all relate to. Champions or not, it's been a hell of a season.'

'I now have the chorus of "The Climb" stuck in my head,' Quinn remarks.

'Let the lyrics inspire you,' Coach says, before pointing at the door. 'Get out there before I get carried away and force you to sing it a cappella.'

Laughter rings through the changing room as the team files out. I linger behind as everyone else leaves. Coach waits for the last person to go and then turns to me.

'Good speech,' I tell him.

He fixes me with a hard stare. 'You ready for another one? Sadie McGrath, you are the most naturally talented player I've ever coached. I will not rest until I see you signed for a club. Even if it takes the next two years of your time at Durham, I am going to work unbelievably hard to get you on the right path. Is that clear?'

'Yes, Coach. Thank you.'

'Don't thank me – it's my job,' he says, his brow furrowed. 'But in return, I need you to do something for me.'

'Please don't ask me to sing Miley Cyrus.'

'I want you to stop *overthinking*. You're a brilliant player for a coach to work with. You follow direction, you're open to trying out different strategies, you are dependable. The scout sitting in the stand knows that. You've proven that side of things. Now he's looking for something else. Something magical.'

I look down at the floor. 'What if I don't have anything magical?'

'You do,' he insists. 'Remember what I told you? It comes when you trust your instincts and play with your heart.'

I sigh. 'Yeah, well, I'm not sure I know how to do that.'

'I thought you might say that, so I thought I'd bring someone in to have a word with you who might have some tips,' he says.

He moves to the door and opens it, gesturing for someone outside to step in. When Arlo walks in sheepishly, I gasp.

'Don't be too long,' Coach tells him, before he leaves, shutting the door behind him.

A silence hangs between us.

'What . . . what are you doing here?' I stammer.

'Before the game, Coach Hendricks mentioned he might need me to give you some pearls of wisdom at half-time,' he says, offering me a wry smile. 'Okay, those weren't his *exact* words. But he said that your confidence might need a boost and that I should encourage you to take risks. He seems to be under the impression that we bring out the best in each other on the pitch.'

I fold my arms across my chest self-consciously.

He hesitates, before quietly adding, 'I think we bring out the best in each other off the pitch, too.'

'Arlo—'

'Sadie, I owe you an apology and an explanation,' he jumps in, taking a step towards me. 'We don't have much time and I appreciate this might not be the best moment to talk about us, so I'm going to tell you the central point of what I want to say, and then you can tell me if you'd rather we leave it until another time and just talk about football now. Okay?'

'Okay.'

He takes a deep breath. 'So the central point of it all

is that I've fallen for you, Sadie. And I'd like to fight for us.' He pauses, looking at me apprehensively. 'Do you want to talk about this now? Or would you rather we talk later?'

I stare at him, my heart thudding against my chest.

'You . . . what?' I whisper.

'I'm in love with you,' he says softly but surely. 'I can expand or we can talk about the advantages of taking risks in football.'

I can hardly breathe.

'Please expand,' I say, before glancing at the clock on the wall. 'Quickly.'

'Sadie, I'm so sorry for the way I've acted with you. The truth is, I didn't *want* to fall for anyone. That was my plan. Losing Tamy was so unbearably painful that I wanted to protect myself from anything that might hurt me ever again. I couldn't handle anything serious. I could cope with anything fun and trivial, so I made a promise to myself to keep my friendships and relationships that way. I didn't want anything to matter. Because if it mattered and I lost it –' he bites his lip, shaking his head – 'I wouldn't be able to handle it.'

He looks so pained and vulnerable, my instinct is to wrap my arms round him and hold him close, but I can't. He takes a moment to collect himself.

'Then I met you.' His shoulders ease and the corners of his mouth curl into a smile as he fixes his eyes on mine. 'I tried to fight my feelings, but I kept getting drawn back to you. I've never felt like this before. I wanted to be around you all the time. You make me . . . happy.'

I swallow.

'I've made so many mistakes,' he admits, wincing at the recollection. 'I kept trying to distance myself from you. I was trying to persuade myself that my feelings weren't real, but deep down I knew I was lying to myself.' He pauses. 'Then I spoke to Hayley the other day.'

I frown at him. 'About her break-up with Dylan?'

'No, she was more concerned about you,' he reveals. 'She knew you were upset after the Loughborough match and thought that whatever was going on between me and you wasn't helping. She said what she'd told you: that I'd said we weren't serious. She felt bad.'

'Oh.'

'It suddenly made sense. You suddenly shutting me out, saying all that stuff about Ellie—'

'She likes you.'

'I don't like her,' he states. 'Not in that way, anyway. I've told her that.'

'But I saw you together at the Loughborough game.'

'A genuine coincidence. She was there with her teammate to support the first team, and so was I. She's great and we're friends, but she knows it's nothing more.' He gives a wave of his hand. 'But this is nothing to do with her. As soon as I spoke to Hayley, I knew I had to get here to Edinburgh to see you and explain.'

'That's why you got here early,' I surmise, 'but then I told you I didn't want to talk about us.'

'You told me you didn't want to talk about anything important, and this is very important to me,' he asserts. 'But if you'd wanted to talk about me and you, I would have started by apologising for saying a stupid offhand comment to Dylan and Hayley about us not being serious. I would have explained that I only said it to get them off my back – and because I was scared. It was pathetic and cowardly. Admitting how serious I was about you out loud would have made it real. I would have had to admit to myself that I was putting myself out there and lining myself up for a very real and very painful heartbreak if things didn't work out or you didn't feel the same way.'

'And what about now?' I ask quietly.

'Oh, I'm terrified. But just like on the pitch, McGrath, if you always play it safe, you might just miss your chance. Sometimes you have to listen to your heart and take the risk.' His throat bobs as he swallows nervously. 'So, here goes. I'm going for goal: Sadie, when it comes to you, I'm all in.'

I stare at him, my head spinning, my heart racing.

My lips part to respond, but we're interrupted by the door swinging open. Coach Hendricks marches in, tapping his watch.

'It's time,' he announces, putting his hands on his hips. 'Have you made your point, Hudson?'

Arlo nods, not taking his eyes off me. 'Yeah, I think I got it across.'

'Great stuff,' Coach says gruffly. 'Come on, McGrath, out you go. Got a game plan?'

'Yeah, a very simple one,' I say, shooting Arlo a knowing smile as I'm ushered out of the room. 'I'm going for goal.'

CHAPTER TWENTY-SIX

As Edinburgh kick off with a deep pass back to one of their central defenders, I watch Amy sprint towards her, applying pressure straight away, and I know that there's only one option for her opponent – to pass it across the goal to her defensive partner. I don't waste any time. Predicting the pass, I sprint to intercept it, lunging forward and tapping the ball onto my left foot. Twenty-five yards out, the keeper isn't expecting me to take a shot. It's a risky move, but it will catch her off guard.

My heart says to go for it, and I'm finally listening.

The ball soars into the top-left corner of the net.

Goal!

A huge cheer erupts from the stand and I punch the air before Amy and Hayley envelop me in a celebratory hug, both of them screaming in my ear. I can hardly dare to believe that just happened, closing my eyes as my two teammates jump up and down beside me. What a great start to the second half. My heart soaring from the rapturous applause from our fans, I glance over at the sideline to see Arlo watching me with a knowing smile.

'That's our girl!' Jade calls out as we move back into position.

The rest of my team is beaming at me, some of them shaking their heads in joyful disbelief, while the Edinburgh side looks shellshocked. We've emerged from that changing room with a fresh wave of determination and equalised in the first minute of returning to the pitch. We're here to win. They know that now.

'We've got this!' I shout to my team, turning to face them and clapping my hands.

The game continues and our next real chance comes a bit later after we've defended a corner and the ball is headed out the box by Jade to Hayley. We're breaking away and I watch Hayley make a fantastic run down the left wing and put in a long through-ball diagonally across to Alisha on the right. She takes a few paces forward and sends a lofted curling cross floating towards the goal, where I'm waiting. It lands at my feet. Our counter-attack has caught the Edinburgh side off guard and I now have four players closing in on me fast. I don't have time to turn. I spot Hayley at the edge of the box and tap it back to her in the space that's been created by the defenders drawn to me.

She drives it into the top-right corner.

Goal. We're two–one up.

Oh my god.

While the team explodes into cheers and Hayley does a celebratory cartwheel before she's pounced upon by Alisha and Quinn, I look at Coach Hendricks. The corners of his mouth twitch into a smile as he meets my eye and I know we're both thinking the same thing.

We might just do this.

I try not to let that hope cloud my focus and do my

best to stay in the moment as we continue play, but as we near the end of the match, the adrenaline is making my fingers tremble. There's five minutes to go and we are piling on the pressure. Amy has a chance at goal but is held back off the ball in the box when a defender sees her break away and grabs her shirt. Both teams are shouting their opinions at the ref – everyone knows what's at stake here. We're given a penalty. This is on me.

'Just breathe,' Amy whispers to me, squeezing my arm.

I exhale through my mouth, smiling at her gratefully. Having told Amy Mum's short but sage advice earlier in the changing room, I needed the reminder.

Stepping up to take it, I walk to the penalty spot, pick up the ball and place it a couple of centimetres to the left of the spot, where I've put it a thousand times during practice. Silence falls across the pitch, but my ears are ringing with my heart pounding so loud. We may be winning this match, but if I score this goal, then we'll be two goals up. We'll win the league. I feel sick with the pressure, my mind racing with *what ifs*.

What if I miss? What if we lose the league? What if the scout doesn't sign me? What if I mess this up and let my team down? What if I let my dad down, who's up there in the stands watching me right now? I've worked so hard for so long, and suddenly it feels as though it all boils down to this one terrifying moment.

What if I let myself down?

That's when I hear him in my head.

All you have to do is kick the ball, McGrath, Arlo's voice tells me.

My shoulders relax, my breathing slows, my heart steadies. I glance at the goal. I step towards the ball and strike it perfectly with the inside of my foot, aiming for the bottom right-hand corner.

The keeper predicts it and gets the tips of her fingers to the ball, pushing it to the left. The ball hits the post and bounces back into play, straight to an Edinburgh defender, who kicks it as far as possible up the pitch for a throw-in.

The disappointment is so crushing it's almost unbearable. My throat tightens as I watch the ball disappear up the pitch, lowering my head and putting my hands on my hips as the chorus of groans from our supporters ripple across the pitch and tear me apart. My knees wobble as though my legs will give way and I'll crumple to the ground.

But I don't.

Somehow, there's a teeny-tiny bit of strength in me that won't let me fall. Despite the unfortunate outcome of that penalty, I still have a fighting bit of hope. And by some miracle, I don't seem to be the only one.

'Head up, Captain,' Hayley says, rushing past me. 'There's still time to win this league and you haven't shown them half of what you can do yet!'

'There's still time,' I repeat under my breath in the hope that if I say it enough, I'll believe in it. 'There's *still time.*'

We get three and a half minutes of injury time and we don't waste a second of it. I've never seen my team play so brilliantly and aggressively, all in tune with one another, no one showing any hint of giving up. When there can't be more than forty seconds left, I instruct everyone to push up the pitch. No more playing it safe.

'We're going for the win,' I mutter to myself.

A nail-biting Edinburgh attack has thankfully come to nothing and the ball has gone out for a goal kick. Maya kicks the ball long, finding Quinn, who confidently chests the ball down to her feet and passes back to Jade. She's already pushing into a more attacking position and has some space, tapping the ball forward a few paces before she sees Hayley gesturing for a through-ball. Jade doesn't hesitate, passing the ball hard in between two defenders and in front of Hayley's run down the left wing. I glance at the linesman to check she wasn't offside – the flag remains down.

Amy is rushing towards the front post and I hover at the back, waiting for Hayley's ball in. A quick glance back down the pitch reveals Maya has come up to the Edinburgh half and our defensive line is joining me and Amy in the box. They took my instructions seriously.

Hayley whips the ball in. As I move forward to attack the cross, I realise I'm unmarked. I launch myself into the air, twist my body and head the ball down into the bottom-right corner. It's as though I'm watching the ball in slow motion as it hits the grass behind the white painted line.

Goal.

Goal. There's an eruption of noise around me, but I'm too stunned to fully acknowledge what's going on, let alone celebrate. Amy picks me up and swings me around before the rest of the team piles in to hug me.

We go through the motions of Edinburgh kicking off before the whistle blows almost immediately. The Durham supporters go wild in the stand. My team are dancing around the pitch in celebration. Coach Hendricks is punching the air and yelling, 'GET IN!'

I stand where I am in the middle of the pitch, breathing heavily and taking it all in. It's a moment I know I will never forget. The moment our team won the league and made history. A moment I know Dad is witnessing and will mean the world to him. The moment I realise that even if we'd lost this match and I'd had to deal with that disappointment, I still wouldn't want to do anything else with my life.

This is it. This is me.

All I have to do is kick the ball.

CHAPTER TWENTY-SEVEN

I'm knocked out of my daze by Jade, who sprints towards me and leaps into my arms, screaming, 'WE WON THE LEAGUE!' at the top of her lungs. Tears of joy filling my eyes, I burst out laughing and start jumping up and down with her before we're joined by Quinn and Alisha, the four of us, arms wrapped around each other, jumping in celebration. Soon, Hayley joins along with Maya, and before we know it, the whole team has piled in. Durham supporters have flooded onto the pitch and everyone is going wild.

Eventually, I pull away from my teammates and scan the sea of faces surrounding us on the field, searching for my parents. I spot them still in the stand, Mum clapping loudly, her cheeks flushed, and Dad next to her, grinning broadly. Breaking away from my team, I weave my way off the pitch and up the steps to get to them. Mum throws her arms round me, before cradling my face in her hands.

'You did it!' she squeals. 'I knew you would!'

'Thanks, Mum. I'm so glad you were here to see it.'

'Wouldn't have missed it for the world,' she whispers, hugging me again.

She steps aside so I can get to Dad.

'Sadie,' he begins, his voice croaky and shaking.

He can't seem to find the words, but it doesn't matter. I step forward to hug him, holding him close and resting my head against his shoulder. Squeezing me so tight it hurts, he kisses the top of my hair. It's a few moments before he lets me go and, as I pull away, he grips my shoulders and looks at me straight on, pressing his lips together, his eyes glistening. He nods sharply and drops his hands, and I know he's fighting back tears.

'You should go celebrate with your team,' Mum says, rubbing my arm. 'I'm guessing you're gearing up for a big night out.'

'It's the men's game next, so we'll stick around for that, and then probably head out together,' I tell her.

Her eyes light up. 'Oh! So Arlo will be there. Tell him he's welcome at ours any time.'

'I will,' I promise. 'If I'm honest, Mum, I think you'll be seeing a lot more of Arlo. You'll be pleased to hear that your ever-so-subtle matchmaking ploy yesterday actually helped.'

She looks at me innocently. 'What matchmaking ploy?'

'Sending me off to be his tour guide,' I say, arching my brow. 'Making up that stuff about me wanting to get some fresh air before today. Inviting him for dinner.'

'I don't know what you're talking about,' she insists.

'McGrath!' Coach barks from the pitch. He gestures for me to come join him.

He's standing with a man I don't recognise.

'Who's that with your coach?' Mum asks curiously.

I swallow the lump in my throat, a rush of nerves flooding my body and making my fingers tingle. 'I . . . I think that might be the scout.'

'Oh. You'd better not keep them waiting. It's all right, Sadie. We're all right here behind you,' she reminds me, before giving me a prod in the back.

As I make my way back down the steps of the stand and onto the pitch towards them, I glance at Arlo. He knows exactly what's going on and gives me an encouraging nod.

Just breathe.

I jump at the chorus of pops from the champagne bottles as Dylan and Quinn stand on top of bar stools, spraying the bubbles over both teams crowded in the private area of the pub that the coaches booked out for us. Coach Hendricks and Coach Nevile are sitting at the bar pretending not to know us as we cheer loudly, soaked from the champagne that Dylan is currently chugging from the bottle. The bar manager gives us a pointed look, but obviously can't be bothered to come over to tell us to calm down – that, or he can see there's no point in attempting to squash our soaring spirits.

The men's team won their game, a brilliant victory sealed by a beautiful goal by Michael with an assist from Arlo. Our team stayed on to watch their match before heading to the pub early while the men's team got changed, which means that I haven't actually spoken to Arlo properly yet. He had just got to the pub and was making his way towards me when the champagne-spraying fun began, becoming temporarily obstructed by the rest of his team.

'I think the first sip of this bottle should go to our captain,' Quinn announces from atop the stool, holding the bottle above her head, the liquid running over her fingers. 'She has led us to a history-making victory – champions three years in a row, baby!'

I blush furiously as everyone cheers, and Quinn jumps down onto the floor. The crowd parts to let her through to me. She hands over the bottle and I take a swig from it, prompting another round of whoops and whistles, before I pass it back to her. She moves away to reveal Arlo right behind her.

'I see Dylan got you good,' I say with a laugh, glancing down at the wet shirt plastered to his muscled torso. 'Remind me to thank him.'

'You didn't get off so lightly yourself,' he counters,

reaching out to brush away the wet lock of hair that's sticking to my cheek. 'Reminds me of that time we got caught in the pouring rain walking back to your college.'

'And now we're soaked in champagne. Look how far we've come.'

He chuckles. As Dylan starts leading everyone in some kind of victory chant and we're jostled by our friends dancing and singing along, Arlo takes my hand and leads me away from them. When he can't find a quiet, unoccupied corner of the pub, he pushes through the doors out into the evening air. Coach Hendricks chose a pub right in the city centre of Edinburgh and the streets are bustling with people.

'So,' Arlo begins, lowering his voice in case anyone we know is lurking out here too, 'what did he say?'

'What did who say?' I ask innocently.

'You *know* who,' he says, frowning impatiently. 'After your match, what happened? I can't believe you refused to tell me until now. Do you know how difficult it was to play with that on my mind?'

'It didn't seem to affect your performance. Congratulations on the win, by the way. I'm glad that the Durham men's team will not be relegated and you can—'

'Sadie,' he interrupts in a warning growl, 'if you don't tell me what you talked about with the scout, I'm going to lose my mind. You've made me wait long enough. *What did he say?*'

I grin up at him, the excitement bubbling up through my body as I speak, hardly daring to believe that what I'm saying is true.

'He said,' I begin slowly and quietly, 'that Manchester United would be interested in having a conversation with me about my future.'

Arlo's eyes widen, his mouth dropping open.

'*Manchester United*,' he breathes. 'Are you serious?!'

'I'm serious,' I confirm, my jaw aching from smiling so much, before adding quickly, 'But don't tell anyone else. I don't want to say anything just in case it doesn't work out.'

'It will work out,' he says matter-of-factly. 'Trust me, Sadie, it will work out.' He bites his lip, shaking his head as he breaks into a smile, his eyes gleaming at me. 'You are *amazing*.'

'I owe a lot of it to you,' I insist. 'He mentioned that I played particularly well after half-time. Apparently, he sensed that my state of mind shifted and that was when I showed my true potential. You can take a lot of the credit for that – not all of it, though. Coach Hendricks and his Miley Cyrus reference also helped.'

'Really? That's interesting,' Arlo says, the corners of his mouth twitching into a playful smile. 'So what you're saying is, to play to your absolute best, you need me?'

'I don't believe those were my exact words.'

'All right, since you asked so nicely, I'll continue to give up my time to be your practice partner and soccer muse. You're welcome.'

'You're insufferable.'

'Yeah, well, you know how you bring out the best in me.'

I hesitate, before saying gently, 'Likewise.'

It has given him the permission he was looking for. He steps closer, sliding his hands round my waist to the small of my back, pressing me into him and forcing me to rest the palms of my hands against his chest and lift my chin to look up. I feel breathless wrapped in his safe, strong arms, a tingling sensation rushing through my body at his warm touch.

'By the way,' I begin, gazing up into his sparkling brown eyes, 'I've been meaning to thank you for pouring your heart out to me in the changing room earlier.'

'You're welcome. As my official mentor, did you have any comments?' he asks, his voice low and raspy as he bows his head, his mouth lightly brushing against my temple. 'Some guidance or advice perhaps?'

'Oh, just one little note.'

'Mm?' he murmurs against my skin. 'Shoot.'

'You were right to take the risk,' I tell him, goosebumps covering my skin. 'With you, Arlo, I've been all in right from the start.'

Emitting a satisfied sigh, his lips find mine and he kisses me, the sort of long, deep kiss that makes the rest of the world around you fade away into the distance. As he eventually breaks away to leave a trail of gentle kisses along my cheekbone and whisper that he loves me into my ear, I close my eyes and exhale, giddy with happiness.

For the first time in a long time, I'm not worrying about the future or overthinking all the possibilities of what's to come. I'm done playing it safe. I'm losing myself in the moment.

I'm finally following my heart.

EPILOGUE

As I finish tying my hair up, I slide up the zip of my hoodie and check how I look in the full-length mirror in my bedroom. I take a deep breath, exhaling slowly, giving myself a moment to pause. I certainly look the part. From a quick glance at me, you wouldn't necessarily be able to tell that my stomach is twisting in knots and my hands are trembling.

It's good to be nervous on a match day. That's what Mum has always said, first to Dad, and now to me.

'You've got this,' I whisper to my reflection.

My first match with Manchester United WFC. Playing for the Reds is a dream come true, and no matter what happens today, I'm grateful to have got this far.

This is it.

Turning away from the mirror, I pick my bag up from the top of the bed and sling it over my shoulder before leaving my room to go into the kitchen where my phone and keys are sitting on the table. Although this flat is small, I love it, and it's in Deansgate, right in the centre of Manchester, a great location for getting anywhere around the city, including training practices. There's also lots of nice cafes on my doorstep, which are perfect to work in when I don't fancy sitting at home alone researching essays. I'm still determined to finish my degree, and Durham made it easy for me to switch to a part-time course.

My phone vibrates with a WhatsApp and a quick glance at the screen reveals that it's Jade, so I hastily open it. She's sent me a photo, a selfie of her with my mum and dad, all three of them smiling at the camera, sitting in their swanky hotel restaurant. A message quickly follows it:

Jade

Grabbing a bite to eat before the
big game!

We'll see you there, so proud of you

Good luck xxxx

P.S. Our seats are VIP, right?!

I chuckle, sending her some heart emojis in response and assuring her that they have good seats, before realising the time and throwing my phone into my bag as I rush to leave the flat, locking it up behind me.

Pushing through the doors of my building, I glance up, expecting to see the car I'd ordered waiting to take me to Leigh Sports Village, but stop in my tracks when I see Arlo straight ahead of me leaning back against a sleek black Mercedes parked out front.

'What are you doing here?' I splutter, my heart skipping at the sight of him. 'I thought I was seeing you after the game.'

'Did you really think I was going to let anyone else drive you to your first ever pro match?' he counters, whipping off his Wayfarers and shooting me a grin.

Dropping my bag to the ground, I run at him, flinging my arms round his neck and closing my eyes as I breathe in his scent. I've never been happier to see him. I move to cradle his face in my hands and kiss him, his arms wrapped round my waist.

'Thank you,' I whisper, our noses still touching.

'How are you feeling?' he asks, his hands resting on my hips.

'Shall we drive to the airport and fly to Hawaii? I think it's a good time for a holiday.'

He chuckles. 'That nervous, huh?'

'What if I make a mistake and let down all the fans?'

'You're not going to make a mistake. You're going to be brilliant. I know it.'

'Easy for you to say.' I sigh, fiddling with the collar of his shirt as he holds me in his strong grip. 'You scouts get to stand there on the sideline, sipping coffee and judging everyone.'

He grins. 'That's funny – that's *exactly* what they teach us on the course. In fact, the entire first module is just on where to find the best coffee to drink on sidelines.'

In spite of the teasing, Arlo knows how proud I am of him taking his first steps towards a career as a professional football scout. It was Coach Hendricks who first suggested the idea to him, the night we won the final in Edinburgh, and ever since then, Arlo couldn't get it out of his head. He's completed his first course and is currently working on the next level. The Manchester United WFC scout who spotted me has offered Arlo the chance to shadow him to get some proper experience. He can't wait to learn the ropes, and seeing him so passionate and excited about a future in football means everything, and not just to me, but to his family, too – his mum flew over to visit recently and she was so proud of him. We're going to be spending a couple of weeks in San Francisco with her next summer.

'In all seriousness, you know you'll be great today,' he continues, moving his hands to grasp my shoulders firmly as he looks me right in the eye. 'If you make a mistake, it doesn't matter. You learn from it and come out fighting next game. We're all human, Sadie, even football players.'

I nod. 'I know. You're right.'

'Most of the time. You ready to go?'

'Ready as I'll ever be,' I say, stepping back as he opens the passenger door for me. 'Nice ride, by the way.'

'Thanks, thought I'd splash out on the car hire for the occasion,' he says with a mischievous glint in his eye. 'I don't know whether you know, but my super-hot girlfriend is the star striker for Manchester United. She deserves to travel in style.'

Laughing, I slide in and wait for him to shut the door behind me and then run round to the driver's seat. He turns down the radio and clips in his belt.

'Oh, before I forget, I've got a bet going with Dylan,' he says breezily, turning on the engine. 'He bet me that you would score in your first ever pro game.'

I frown. 'And you bet *against* that?'

'I bet that you'd score two,' he says with a grin, sliding on his sunglasses.

'Two goals in my first pro game,' I say, leaning back in my seat and smiling as we pull away to head towards the stadium. 'That sounds like a challenge.'

Acknowledgements

Special thanks to the fabulous Yas, the most wonderful, sunshiney editor. Working on this project with you was so much fun, thank you for all your guidance and encouragement, and for entrusting me with this – I feel so lucky that we get to work together! Thank you to the talented team at Simon and Schuster for all your hard work on this book, and to XX for the beautiful cover art and XX for the fantastic cover design.

Huge thanks to Lauren, Callen and everyone at my agency, you are my rocks, and I couldn't do any of this without you. Same goes to my family and friends, you know who you are.

A great big thank you to Fionn, Woody and Ben, my

football gurus. It was great fun chatting the details of play through with you and I am ever impressed by your extensive knowledge of the beautiful game – you guys are the best.

Thank you so much to the readers of *Playing the Field*. Sport has an amazing way of bringing people together, no matter who you are, and this book has been created to honour that. Whether you're out on the pitch playing football, or cheering on your team, I hope that those exhilarating moments bring you joy, excitement, celebration and hope – as Sadie's dad says, each game is a new game.

And lastly, Up The Villa.